THE HIGHLANDS TRILOGY

JOHN A. THOUMIRE

Printed in the United Kingdom

Wildwoods Publishing
40 Angle Park Terrace
Edinburgh, Scotland

TABLE OF CONTENTS

ACKNOWLEDGMENTS

There are entirely too many that deserve thanks when it comes to this book. In particular I'd like to dedicate this title to my family:

To Mum and Dad for giving me the will never to give up. To my brother Simon for the fantastic advice and for getting me off my behind. To Laurs for all the laughs.

To Pete, whose kidney (now mine) kept me going when my own turned to cottage cheese.

Finally, to my simply wonderful wife Eleisha. Without you I wouldn't have gotten past the first page.

RED SKY AT NIGHT

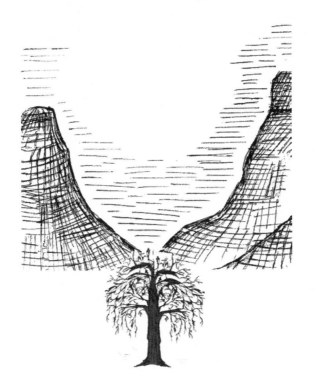

<u>1</u>

Black clouds rampaged across the scarlet sky. He stood beneath a dark tree with no leaves; it was his only way back to the world he knew. What was this place? Why did it burn his skin?

A familiar voice called out his name but there was nobody there. He was alone in this world.

The giant tree was the last tie to his old life. The limbs that once reached out to him now hung limp and lifeless. Little more than kindling. Thunder cracked overhead, threatening rain that would never come.

'Tom…'

He knew not to look for it.

In the distance he could see fire racing towards him, but he couldn't do anything. Why wasn't he doing anything?

The ground shook as another blast of lightning struck, and he fell to his knees. The fire was almost on him now. He waited for it to take him…

2

Tom woke up covered in sweat, bed-clothes clinging to him. His heart was beating hard. The blankets were wrapped around, trapping his legs. Not that it mattered.

Beside the bed, a machine was alarming - the dialysis machine. Tom grabbed at the tube running from him to it. The pipe had kinked, restricting the fluid from draining out of him. He straightened it out, hit the reset button and waited for it to start working again – a slow, steady sucking noise rhythmically flowing from the man to machine.

Tom lay back down, his breathing ragged.

The dream felt so real this time. It was getting more detailed.

'Do you want to talk about it?'

His wife Lisa lay on one elbow facing him, a worried look on her face.

He took a towel down from the headboard and wiped the sweat from his face. He was surprised at how damp it came away.

'Just a bad dream, that's all…'

'The same one?'

'Yes and no… I'm not sure. I can't really remember now. They fade so fast'

Tom lay back down. The machine was nearing the end of its cycle, his stomach strained against it, making him wince.

Every night he had to hook up to it. Over eight hours it went through the process four times. *Drain. Fill. Dwell. Drain. Fill. Dwell.* If he woke up at the wrong time, he could feel his stomach shrivelling to the size of a walnut.

'Are you going to town tomorrow?' he asked Lisa.

'Mmm?' she moaned.

Lisa was already falling back asleep. That was good; he didn't like her losing sleep because of him.

Tom rolled onto his side and looked out the window.

The wind rattled the shutters outside.

He'd lied to Lisa. He never forgot the dreams. They were etched onto his mind.

They'd begun when he first started on dialysis. He would wake up sweltering three or four times a night. The nurses had said to expect some side effects so he hadn't worried about it.

That was six months ago. He hardly ever slept now, if he did, it was in his wheelchair in front of the TV.

Nine months ago their car had spun off the road into s tree. Lisa got away with a fractured arm. Tom wasn't so lucky. He'd been thrown out of the front windscreen, both legs broken and ruptured kidneys. The legs were healing, the kidneys were shot.

The doctors said it would be between three and five years before a transplant came his way.

It was Lisa who decided that they needed a fresh start. They moved up north to the Highlands, far from Edinburgh, rented a house and workshop and had been trying since then to build a new life. She designed jewellery, he did his best to make it.

The location was off the beaten track but still good for the business - just outside Aviemore - a major tourist haunt – and with a spectacular view of the Cairngorm mountain range.

Mostly they kept to themselves. They were far enough away from the town to not attract many visitors at home. Tom wasn't a big fan of visitors.

Branches outside scraped the window, their shadows passing over the bed like a clawing hand. Out in the garden, an ancient oak looked like the one from his dream. Its tall, dark trunk leaned away from the house but its arms stretched over the roof. Tom spent most evenings trying not to look but it was hard to miss.

They'd asked if it could be trimmed back but the landlord had said it was protected. Apparently it was one of the oldest trees in the area and held a certain significance.

On the last day of April in 1690, the surviving soldiers from the Battle of Cromdale, the final nail in the coffin of the Jacobite rebellion, made it back as far as the area. They made camp around the tree but were caught unawares by the enemy. They were slaughtered where they slept.

Some say if you looked close enough, you could still see marks of battle on the wood. Tom could never see any though.

He tried to flex his legs but the pain ratcheted up his body. They told him he was healing, that the pain would subside and he'd be walking in no time. None of that mattered when he lay in bed, tied to the machine. The display on the front of the unit glowed a sickly green in the darkness:

'Dwell 1 of 4'

It meant he had a couple of hours respite before the drain cycles started again. He rubbed where the tube went into his stomach and coiled just beneath the surface before entering his peritoneum.

In the dream he didn't have any of this stuff. His legs were fine and he wasn't tied to the unit, but he was alone.

He'd tried looking into it himself, reading dream books etc. He'd even talked to a medium to see if they could shed some light on it. Nobody knew. They all thought it sounded like hell though.

Tom closed his eyes; he was back in the dream. The sky had turned blood red and the earth was scorched. Like an old river bed the land spread out in front of him, dead and lifeless.

The tree towered over him, its branches spanning for miles. There was an opening in the trunk, big enough to walk through and bark framed it like a lintel. Was it the way home?

When he opened his eyes, his heart was racing again. The dream had changed. He had never noticed the opening in the tree before. He sat up to see the sun rising over the mountains, morning rays hitting the snow on top. Frost clung to the branches outside the window, icy droplets reflecting light into the bedroom.

Tom picked up a book and waited for the machine to finish its work for the night. The usual routine.

He'd disconnect, go through and have a coffee.

The usual routine.

He'd go to the workshop and try to forget the dreams.

The usual routine.

3

Tom sat in his wheelchair by the workbench. He tried to bend the silver wire to a shape Lisa had drawn the day before but the metal was cold, coiling back to its original form. Tom pushed it away in exasperation. Better to try later when things had warmed up a bit.

He wheeled himself through to the kitchen and poured another cup of coffee. Lisa sat in the other room with a pad of paper designing more work for him.

'Coffee?' he called through.

He heard the pad hit the table in the living room, his wife came to the kitchen and leaned over, kissing him on the cheek. She wore an orange silk scarf that used to belong to her grandmother.

'No thanks, any more and I'll sleep as well as you do.'

She stepped behind him, pushed the wheelchair towards the kitchen table, and took a seat beside him.

'That wire isn't wanting to play today,' he said.

'I'm not surprised,' she laughed. 'It's bloody freezing in there. Have you tried the solder?'

'No, I'd rather let it come to on its own. Also it gives me an excuse to come and see you.'

'Aww, aren't you sweet,' she laughed again, then leaned back and took his hand.

'Do you want come into town with me, I've a couple of things to do but we could go for a coffee after?'

Tom leaned over and kissed her on the cheek.

'Not today sweets.'

Disappointment flashed across her eyes.

'You're becoming known as the hermit down there you know, the fabled elf who does all the work but won't show his face.'

He smiled.

'You can tell them I live in the tree and only come out at night.'

'As you wish sir.'

He wheeled himself over to the back door.

'Would you like to accompany me on a short tour of the grounds before you visit the masses?'

His wife stood up and bowed in agreement. She opened the door and pushed the chair down the ramp.

Outside the air was crisp, their breath frosted in front of them.

They took the same path every morning, meandering past the cottage and through the garden, finishing by the giant oak. Tom stopped and faced the view of the mountains, it was magnificent. But Lisa was looking at the tree.

'Have you ever noticed that before?' she asked, bending towards the oak. 'There's a crack in the trunk, look.'

Tom turned the wheelchair to face the tree.

'I don't see anything…'

'Here,' she said pointing.

He looked closer, she was right. There was a crack running down from the middle of the trunk down to the roots. It was barely noticeable at the top but by the time it reached the bottom it was wide enough to stick a hand though.

Tom thought back to his dream the night before.

'I think we should call the landlord about this,' said Lisa, 'If this oak is going to fall,

I don't want the locals at us with pitchforks saying we destroyed their sacred tree.'

Tom nodded, his mind still on the dream. The doorway.

'I'll call him this afternoon.'

'There's no way we're paying for this.'

'Calm it dear, I'm sure we won't be expected to pay and if we are… we're using it for firewood.'

When the landlord arrived that afternoon in his four-wheel drive behemoth, Tom could hear the engine revving all the way from the house.

Callum Grimmond was a rotund gentleman who wore a tweed suit and a self-important swagger. Grimmond owned several properties in the area and was well known for making himself heard if he wasn't happy with any given situation. Tom didn't particularly like him.

17

'So lad, what have you got to show me?'

He bellowed the words before he was even out of the car.

'Come and see for yourself,' Tom shouted back.

Grimmond strutted out in front of Tom, never offering to help with the wheelchair. He took in the house as he walked, looking for any signs of misuse on the couple's part.

'That oak is hundreds of years old you know. Means a lot to this community. People's kin died around this old oak.'

'Yes we know,' replied Tom, 'that's why I called you right away.'

Tom watched as the landlord waddled over to the tree, he leaned in and inspected the cleft trunk.

'You've only seen this today, aye?' he grunted.

'Yes, this morning.'

'... And you didn't touch it?'

'No Mr Grimmond, we didn't touch the tree' said Tom. 'My wife and I came out for a walk this morning and she noticed the crack in the trunk. Two hours later, I called you and now here you are.'

Green looked at Tom suspiciously, unsure if he was being made fun of.

'I'll have someone round tomorrow,' he said turning back towards the path. 'Will you be in?'

Tom knocked the arm of his wheelchair.

'More than likely.'

Without waiting he walked back along the path and out of sight.

Tom arrived back in time to hear the car's ignition burst into life. It turned and left the drive, showering him in gravel. He was sure it was intended.

Back inside, Tom wheeled himself over to the bathroom. He washed his hands in the sink for five minutes - another of his daily practices. He had to be as clean as possible before touching the machine. He couldn't risk infecting the various lines that connected him to the bags of glutinous liquid.

He stared out the window at the oak while he rinsed his hands. Every now and then the breeze would scrape its branches across the pane, making his skin crawl.

Tom was still getting used to the silence of their new home. He kept expecting to hear a car horn or police siren in the distance. He remembered the first time they'd heard a fox outside, neither of them had slept another wink that night.

Mostly they heard the wind.

He finished setting up the machine and was cleaning up the copious amount of rubbish that came with the operation when he heard a noise above him.

They had trouble with rats when they first moved in. It had taken weeks to get Grimmond to send somebody to sort it out.

Tom stopped and listened for more rustling but there was nothing. The house was silent. He looked out the window to see nothing but clouds skimming across the sky.

Anything broken on the roof would mean another call to the landlord and he really didn't want that.

He heard it again - a strange popping, like fire crackers going off.

Tom put down the bag of rubbish and moved to the centre of the room. He looked up. There was a crack in the ceiling but that had been there since they'd moved in.

He listened as the noise began to move out of the room. For a second he thought he heard somebody shouting too.

He left the room and went into the kitchen. They seemed to be heading outside. Tom followed in his wheelchair. Confused, he opened the back door. The noises stopped immediately.

Outside he could see Lisa was pulling up in the driveway.

'Alright?' she shouted from the car.

'Not sure. Can you see anything on the roof?'

Lisa left the car and walked along the length of the house, looking up.

'Why, what's wrong?'

'I was sure I heard something from inside.'

His wife bent down and kissed him.

'It was probably just a cat.

Tom looked back at the roof.

'Yeah, you're probably right. Just a little strange, that's all.'

4

Tom stood in front to the tree again, the sky burned red over his head. He could never seem to remember how he got there.

He was standing next to his wheelchair. His legs felt fine.

He looked over his shoulder. The machine lay behind him, threatening to remind him of reality. It was surrounded by flames. He felt for the tube in his stomach. That too had gone. He almost felt like smiling.

A peel of thunder brought him back. Dark clouds circled the top of the tree, its branches swaying back and forth.

'Here…'

The voice came from behind him but he never turned.

Tom took a step forwards, the hole in the tree looked even more like a doorway this time.

It reminded him of something he'd seen recently, he couldn't put his finger on it, something about the tree and the door… no crack. The image slipped away.

'Here…'

He looked up, this was different.

'What is this?' he said into the air.

Tom winced as his stomach cramped, he turned round. His dialysis machine was on fire, the bags on top boiled in their cases. He tried to beat out the flames, instead they rose higher, the plastic casing of the machine began to melt.

Tom fell to his knees grasping his stomach. Smoke seeped out of the wound where the tube should have been.

He lifted his head. Dark eyes stared out at him from the door in the tree.

5

Tom woke, morning sunlight streamed in through the window past the shadow of the tree.

The machine sat silently next to him. 'Therapy Complete' blinked at him from the display. His stomach felt tender, the fluid settling inside. The details of the dream replayed over and over. The fire. The pain. The eyes.

'Tom…'

He rolled over. Lisa was just waking next to him.

'Morning sweets,' he whispered to her.

'What time is it?' she asked sleepily.

'Don't worry, it's Saturday. Sleep as long as you want.'

She smiled. Tom could see her already sinking back into the pillows.

Disconnecting from the machine, he pushed himself through to the kitchen. The whole house felt cold this morning.

Tom looked at the clock on the wall. It was just after 9:00. He was going to make breakfast in bed for Lisa, scrambled eggs on toast - her favourite. It was likely to be a lazy weekend for them. There wasn't a whole lot to do for someone in a wheelchair round there and he knew his wife wouldn't want to leave him on his own for the day.

He felt bad for that. He never really left the house. It was embarrassing how tired he got these days. More often than not, they would have to cut short any plans they made because he'd be exhausted or Lisa would worry because he may get that way. He promised himself he'd make it up to her when he was well again, that once out of the chair he'd have his energy back.

Tom hoped he could keep that promise.

He was thinking of things for them to do that day when heard a low rumble.

Outside dark clouds were gathering on the mountains. Tom turned on the laptop and checked the weather forecast. Heavy rain was predicted for the afternoon with snow flurries on Sunday. Tom sighed. He hated snow.

An hour later he was still trying to make breakfast when Lisa came into the room, wrapped up in a thick woollen jumper.

'I wouldn't make any plans to take that off anytime soon,' said Tom.

She glanced at the weather page, then walked over to the thermostat on the wall and turned it up to full.

'I'm not leaving this spot until June.'

Tom laughed and slid over some scrambled eggs on toast.

Over food they decided that the day would best be served on the sofa watching movies and occasionally napping. It sounded perfect.

They were all ready to begin when they heard a noise over their heads, Lisa looked at Tom. It started again, it sounded like somebody coughing.

'Is that the noise you heard yesterday?' said Lisa.

'Not really,' he replied.

Lisa helped him off the sofa into the wheelchair and they went out to the front garden.

A dirty white transit van was parked in the driveway, its rear doors open. Inside were a collection of rusty saws and wide leather belts.

They looked at each other confused.

'Don't touch those,' shouted a voice from behind.

They were surprised to see a skinny little man clinging to their chimney, waving an arm wildly at them.

'That's specialist stuff, leave it alone'.

They retreated from the van to the lawn.

'Who the hell are you?' Tom shouted 'What the hell are you doing on our roof?'

The young man didn't answer. He disappeared to the other side of the house and emerged a few seconds later coming round from the back garden.

He walked over and stood in front of them.

'Grimmond asked me to come over and take a look at your tree, he said it was urgent.'

He spoke to them like you would a child. Tom could feel his wife winding up next to him.

'And your name is?' she asked.

'Danny. I deal with all his properties.'

He looked to be in his early twenties and wore a pair of dirty green overalls over a football top. A baseball cap was perched on top of his head, a wispy ponytail poking out the back.

'Didn't you think it appropriate to call ahead? It's a Saturday after all.'

'Not really' he said. 'When Mr Grimmond says something is urgent I believe him. Besides, he never said anybody would be in.

Danny glanced down at the wheelchair and smirked.

'I guess he was wrong.'

Tom took his wife's hand and squeezed it to calm her. Clearly there was going to be no arguing with this one.

'How long is this likely to take?' asked Tom.

'No idea mate,' he replied looking back at the house. 'I was disturbed before I even got a look at a branch.'

'Sweets' said Tom to Lisa, 'why don't you go in and relax, I'll be in back in a few minutes.'

She bent down and kissed him on the lips, she gave the Danny one last stony glare before going back into the house.

'Come on then' he said to Danny, 'let's get this over and done with.'

He walked alongside Tom.

'I didn't mean to offend your wife mate, I was just doing as I was told. Honest, Mr Grimmond never said anyone would be here. He even gave me a key to make myself some tea.'

'Best you don't let yourself in the house for the moment Danny. I can't promise what my wife will do. If you want a cup of something, talk to me.'

'Cool, I'll do as you say... Why are you in the chair?' he asked suddenly.

The question caught Tom off-guard; he was used to people pussy-footing around it, unsure if it was touchy subject or not.

'An accident about a year ago. Broke both my legs and left me in this.'

He tapped the chair.

'Is it permanent?'

'Hopefully not. The doctors say I'll be walking again in six months or so.'

'Lucky it was just your legs huh?'

Tom grunted in agreement, the tube in his stomach telling another story.

They came to the tree round the other side of the house.

He couldn't be sure but the crack was looking bigger, wider.

Danny walked over for a closer look, then took a measuring tape out of his pocket and held it up against the trunk.

'You said you handled all Grimmond's properties' said Tom. 'Doing what?'

Danny continued to measure as he spoke.

'Oh, this and that. Mostly maintenance work. Yesterday I was fixing the roof on one of his lofts on the other side of town.'

'So you're not a tree surgeon or anything? asked Tom.

'A what? I don't think so. If you're looking for a piece of paper to saying so though, I'll print one out for you later.

Tom laughed. He was starting to like the young man.

'I'm off inside,' he said 'If you need anything give a knock on the door.'

'Righto. See if you can get your wife to stop sharpening her knives while you're at it.'

'Easier said than done'

Inside he found Lisa in a heated exchange over the phone.

'…It's Saturday morning for god's sake. Could it not wait until Monday? I understand the historical significance but if it falls on the bloody house…'

Tom left her to it and hoped she wouldn't get them evicted.

Outside he could see Danny walking over to his van where pulled out two large leather straps and hung them over his shoulder.

'What's he doing now? Lisa was off the phone. She was red in the face from shouting.

'I'm not exactly sure he knows what he's doing but I think he's not that bad a guy. Grimmond on the other hand… What was he saying?'

'Same old shit.' She said flopping down onto the sofa.

Tom knew she was annoyed; she rarely swore.

'Let him fix it then,' he said 'So long as we're not footing the bill, let them do whatever they want.'

He looked out at the tree for a few minutes before going back to the sofa. Tom stayed

in his chair in case Danny came to the
door.

<u>6</u>

They'd barely watched half a movie before the rain began to pour, outside quickly became a mud track and they heard a knock at the door.

Danny stood there, a ripped bin bag over his head and shoulders.

'That's all I'll be doing for today mate, I'll be back in a few days to check on the things. If you notice any changes for the worse, give me a bell.'

He handed over a torn piece of paper with a number scribbled over it.

'Oh, I'm not going to say anything to Grimmond about the graffiti. He's got a thing for that tree. I figure he'll tear into all of us if he finds out.'

'What graffiti?' Tom asked confused.

'Whatever mate,' said Danny smiling through the rain. 'If Grimmond sees your name cut into that wood, you'll be paying for it. I promise you that.'

He turned and ran back through the rain to his van, his ponytail dripping down his back.

Tom watched as the transit turned and headed back down to the main road, red brake lights disappearing into the rain.

Tom went back to the living room. He sat silently for a few minutes thinking about what Danny had said.

Outside the rain was torrential. The wheelchair slipped and slid down the ramp, pools of water covered the gravel path.

Tom was already regretting this. By the time he'd reached the tree he was soaked through and freezing to the bone. The rain had ignored the rain coat he'd hastily put on before leaving the house. There was nowhere for him to hide and lightning was flickering on the horizon.

Danny had bound the trunk of the tree with the great straps of leather in an attempt to push it back together. Between them a large metal bolt had been hammered through the wood and tightened at both ends.

It all looked wrong. Industry meeting nature; the latter looked to have more strength.

He pushed the wheelchair through the mud of the lawn for a closer look.

He couldn't see any sign of the graffiti. Tom was about to turn back when he noticed a gap between the leather straps, behind them the crack in the tree showed. He leaned in, a flash of lightening erupted behind him. The inside of the tree lit up, and carved clearly on the wood was his name. Deep gauges for each letter.

'Tom'

He pushed back from the tree and wrenched the chair round.

'Who's there?' he shouted into the rain.

Another flash of lightening lit up the area.

The tree began to sway menacingly in the wind, its branches whipping towards him.

He pushed himself back to the house. Round the corner, the flicker from the television through the window caught his eye. Lisa lay asleep on the sofa where he'd left her.

Lightening flashed again. Something else was in the room with her, he was sure of it. It was reaching out to his wife.

The sky flickered around him with another bolt. When he looked back, Lisa was alone again.

Tom pushed at the wheels of the chair as hard as he could. The mud sucked at the tires, slowing him down.

Finally he burst through the door, the pain in his legs excruciating.

'Lisa!' he shouted.

He rushed over to the sofa, where she was stretching her arms, a smile of contentment stretched across her face. Her eyes turned to shock at seeing him. She ran to his side.

'What the hell happened to you?' she said 'You're soaked through.'

Tom waved her aside and moved round the sofa, looking into all the corners.

'What's wrong?' said Lisa. 'What were you doing?'

Tom slumped back into his chair, water dripping from his hair.

'I don't know,' he sighed. 'I went out to check on the tree and I thought I saw something… someone in here with you.'

Lightning lit up the room again.

'… I was so sure…'

Lisa's hug cut him off. She looked him in the eye.

'I'm fine, don't worry' she said 'Thank you for being a hero though. It's always nice to have one around the house. Come on, let's get you dry.'

7

Tom was running across a burning field. The scarlet sky seemed closer than ever, he felt the weight of it bearing down on his shoulders.

This time, something ran alongside him, hidden amongst the flaming grass. Close but out of reach. Visible yet out of sight.

Tom shook his head, trying to clear his mind.

'It's just a dream,' he told himself.

But he kept running.

In the distance he could see the tree, its charcoal black branches stretched out to the sky.

He ran towards it but it never seemed to get any closer.

Its great trunk was achingly close, the only thing in this world he recognised, the only thing solid.

Tom stopped to catch his breath, it all felt so real. The fire around him burned fiercely, the heat blasted all around.

'What are you waiting for?'

Something stood in the grass next to him. He turned quickly but it had already moved.

It now stood off in the distance; a black speck on the charred horizon.

'Was that him?' thought Tom.

'Not this time.' The voice came from over his shoulder. There was something different about it, something sinister. Before, it was without emotion, a noise floating in the ether. Now he could hear malice.

'You know where to find me.'

'What do you want?' asked Tom

Behind him stood the tree, dark and imposing. The doorway in the trunk lay open, a cooling breeze wafted over him from within. It was a welcome reprieve from the scorching heat around.

A reflection of light in the darkness caught his eye, a metallic object. Tom took a step closer. There it was again.

He reached into the doorway, grasping at the object. It was like ice on his skin, whatever it was burnt him with the cold. Tom snatched his hand away and took a step back.

'What are you afraid of?' it said.

Tom looked down at his palm. A line of seared, torn skin ran down its length.

He looked up, something rolled out of the doorway;

It was a wheelchair, his wheelchair.

'What is this?' pleaded Tom, 'please, somebody talk to me'.

Pain exploded in his legs. He fell to the ground, screaming in pain.

The chair moved forwards by itself. He pushed himself away but soon the burning fields of grass were behind him. Trapped.

Flames closed in all around. Tom closed his eyes, his knees felt like they had daggers buried in them.

He braced himself for the worst...

<u>8</u>

A noise above broke the spell. Tom opened
his eyes; it was coming from directly above
them. The same popping sounds he'd heard
earlier that day. Except now they sounded
sharper, like gunfire. He lay still. His
imagination was playing tricks on him. His
breath caught as he heard it again, this time
from another room.

Tom rolled over and unhooked from the
machine. Pulling himself into the
wheelchair he went to the other room.

Out of the darkness he heard a hissing
sound, like static.

Slowly he made his way through the house.
The floorboards creaked as the chair rolled
over them.

From the kitchen he could see the TV, a
steady flicker emanating from the screen;
the only light in the house.

Tom felt a cramp in his stomach.

He heard something smash in the living room, the storm outside suddenly grew louder.

Inside the living room he found the window broken, a branch from the tree stuck through the shattered glass, a pool of water gathering underneath.

'Shit.'

The TV next to him flashed with static. A grainy picture showed between the flickering lines.

'Lisa must have left it on.'

Tom stared at the screen. A burning red sky and a field of flames faded into the screen. It reminded him of the magic eye pictures you'd get in the newspapers. In the midst of the scene stood a cloaked figure.

Tom reached for the remote control, pressed the red power button. Once. Twice. Nothing happened.

The image on the screen sharpened; the cloaked figure seemed to be grinning, shaking his head from side to side.

Tom dropped the remote, moved to the wall and ripped the TV plug from its socket. The screen was still on, the figure still there with its muted grin.

Tom rubbed his eyes.

'It's just a dream,' he told himself. But the cloaked man seemed to be looking right at him. He raised his hand and Tom felt a sudden sting on his palm. He looked down to see a streak of charred skin.

The wheelchair began to shake, as if something had taken hold of it. Tom gripped the wheels but the chair continued to move.

 It started to turn in a circle, faster and faster it spun until it stopped suddenly.

Standing in front of him was a man. It was the figure from the television. His eyes glowed with a dark intensity.

'Who are you?' said Tom from between clenched teeth. His stomach cramping up again 'What are you doing in my home?'

Beneath the cloak, the man wore strange clothes: a loose white shirt with lace ties at the neck, a dark coloured waist coat over the top – the ancient garb of highlanders.

'*Your* home Tom?'

Its voice was dry and rasped as if it hadn't spoken in a long time.

'What do you want?' cried Tom.

Dimly he heard an alarm going off. It was the dialysis machine warning him to reconnect.

Next to him, the TV had started smoking from inside, flames licked at the grey plastic surround. The chair still wouldn't move.

Tom threw himself on to the floor, away from the flames. Pain shot up his legs.

A light in the hallway switched on and then Lisa was next to him, a look of horror on her face.

She ran out and returned seconds later holding a red fire extinguisher. She aimed the canister at the fire and pulled down the handle. The fire disappeared in an explosion of noise and white smoke.

Tom looked around the room, the figure had disappeared. They were alone.

Rain spattered them from the broken window.

'Tom!' cried Lisa. 'What happened?'

He lay there in silence, his breath coming in painful rasps.

She pulled him back into the wheelchair, back to the bedroom and reconnected to the machine.

The cut in his palm. The TV. The window. He couldn't answer anything now. He needed sleep but in the back of his mind he knew something waited for him there too.

He felt trapped all over again.

<u>9</u>

Tom sat in the waiting room of the local GP's surgery on Monday morning.

A mother and her two children sat opposite him. The kids were arguing over a computer game while she read copies of last year's Reader's Digest.

Lisa had insisted on the check-up that morning, he'd rather have left it.

The cut on his hand was already looking better and the pain in his legs had subsided.

He was there for her. Pure and simple.

He'd already been in and out, the doctor had a few pointed questions to ask him but overall he'd agreed there was nothing fatal from the previous night.

After, he'd asked to speak to Lisa on her own for a few minutes. Tom knew how that was going to go.

'What's he been doing?' he'd ask. 'Is he getting out? Is he showing any signs of depression?'

Another excuse to get Tom to take more pills.

He looked down at his bandaged palm.

'What the hell happened last night?' he thought. 'Was it real, did I really see those things? Please don't let me be going crazy'

He clenched his hand, dull pain radiated up his arm. His memory of the night before was still fresh. The TV, the figure, the fear.

Tom looked up as he heard a loud thump across the room. One of the boys had pushed the other over. The tears were already welling up. The other boy looked away trying to avoid his mother's gaze. She put down her magazine and picked the other boy up off the ground, she sat him on her lap and started to sing quietly into his ear.

It was a nursery rhyme.

'Row row row your boat gently down the stream…'

The door opened and Lisa walked out flanked by the doctor, they shook hands and looked down at him. A knowing look passed between them.

'Alright Tom,' said the doctor. I think we'll see you again in a couple of weeks, just to check on how things are going. Ok?'

He felt crushed, only last month the hospital had gauged him well enough to only have an appointment every three months. Now he was back to two weeks.

Back home, Tom went straight to the bedroom and lay down. Lisa followed with a cup of tea.

'Tom. What happened last night?'

The question hung in the air, like a noose from a tree. What would she say if he told

57

her what really happened? If he said
nothing would she worry more?

'I don't know…'

A loud noise came from down the hall.
Somebody was knocking on the front door.

'Hang on,' said Lisa. She got up and ran
down the hall.

Tom sat up and looked out the window;
Danny's white transit van was parked in
the drive way.

He pulled himself into the wheelchair and
went to the kitchen.

The door was open. Lisa and Danny stood
in the garden, deep in a heated
conversation. Danny was pointing at a pile
of thick leather straps on ground.

'What's wrong?' shouted Tom from the
door.

Lisa signalled for him to come outside, her orange scarf flapping wildly in the wind.

The rain had stopped and a crisp wind had set in, he was shivering as he stopped in front of the other two.

Danny pointed again to the leather at his feet.

'You two owe me for this. That's expensive equipment that is.'

Tom looked up in surprise.

'Owe you for what? I'm sorry I don't understand.'

Lisa turned to him.

'He's saying he wants money for a replacement. I'm just telling him that this is a rented house and it's not our responsibility. He needs to talk to Mr Grimmond about it.'

'Mr Grimmond pays me for the job, not the equipment,' explained Danny.

Tom picked up a leather strap from the ground; one end had been sheared off by something sharp.

'Why did you cut them off if you knew you didn't have a replacement?' he asked,

Danny grabbed the leather out of his hands, his palm stung as the strap dragged over the wound.

'But I didn't do this,' Danny said holding up the cut end. 'I came to look at it this morning and found them lying at the bottom of the tree. One of you must have sliced them off and you owe me money for it.'

Tom felt his insides seize.

'Sweets,' he said to his wife 'let's go and take a look eh, I want to see for myself.'

Lisa moved round to the back of the chair and pushed him down the path, Danny followed behind holding what was left of the straps.

They stopped in front of the huge Oak. The crack in the trunk was now wide enough to stick your head through. The metal bolt that had previously been sticking into the wood was now lying on the ground.

Tom ran his hand down the edges of the gap. Inside he could still read his name carved into the wood, Lisa read it and looked at him.

'Very funny Tom' she said 'you know Grimmond is going to use this as an excuse to make us pay for the whole thing.'

Tom wasn't listening, something else had been written in the wood.

'Red sky at night'

'I didn't do this,' he said. 'Not the name, not the words.'

Tom felt his heart pounding.

Lisa and Danny had started arguing again.

The wind seemed to have picked up, he looked at the others but they were busy at each other's throats.

Tom stared at the carvings in the wood.

'Red sky at night'

'Tom… TOM!'

He started, Lisa was shaking his arm. She pointed down the path. Callum Grimmond was striding towards them, his tweed long coat flapping in the wind.

'What's going on here?' he shouted. 'I can hear you from down the road.'

He stopped by the tree.

'Danny, I told you to come and see to this days ago. Is this you just getting to it now?'

'No Mr Grimmond,' said Danny 'I was here on the weekend as you said, I came back today to check up on things but there's been a problem'.

Tom watched as Lisa stepped in front of the landlord.

'There is no problem,' she said 'I was just saying that we're not paying for something that we didn't do.'

'What exactly did you not do?' said Grimmond.

Danny handed him the sheared strap and looked towards the tree.

Grimmond examined the crack. He ran his hands down the side of the tree.

Tom waited for him to mention the writing; it was clearly visible in the daylight.

Grimmond turned back to Danny and took the straps from him. He ran his finger over the end that was cut.

'Danny,' he said 'we need something done about this and these straps aren't going to do it. Go and wait by my car, we'll have a chat about a solution.'

Danny shrugged and walked away.

'Don't worry about the money' he said to Lisa 'this'll take a long time to fix this problem and it wouldn't be fair to put the price to you.'

He turned and studied the tree.

Tom moved over to his wife. She looked at him and nodded, then turned to the landlord.

'Mr Grimmond,' she said 'I'm sorry if I was rude before. We'd just gotten back from a hospital appointment when your man arrived and I think said a few things I shouldn't have.'

He waved his hand dismissively.

'Not to worry, though maybe you should be saying this to Danny and not me. I've grown a thick skin over the years. He's still a young 'un.'

'I suppose you're right, ok.'

Tom watched as Lisa walked back round the house.

The two men were left by themselves.

'You're looking a bit ragged Tom,' said Grimmond. 'Not getting enough sleep?'

Tom looked up. The man had never really spoken to him before now. Let alone asked after his health.

'It's just a bit of an adjustment that's all,' he replied. 'I think I'm still getting used to the silence of this place.'

Grimmond turned and stared into his eyes.

'Are you sure that's all it is?'

Before he could answer, Grimmond had turned back to the great oak.

'There's a lot of history to this tree you know' he said. 'Been around for centuries. My grandfather used to tell us such tales about this place, about strange goings on. For years people were afraid of this whole area, they said it attracted bad elements.

You've heard of the battle?'

Tom nodded.

'Bits and pieces.'

'They say the Jacobite rebellion died here… April of 1690' continued Grimmond. 'The battle started north of here in Cromarty. Most of the Highlanders were killed off in the initial skirmish. The survivors retreated south to here. Unaware that they were being followed, they made camp, apparently round this tree.

'That night, their pursuers encircled the camp and fired on them while they slept.

The Highlanders were slaughtered to a man.

'Witnesses the next morning said that the tree was red from all the blood.'

A gust of wind sent the branches of the oak clacking against each other, their shadows creating a spider's web over their heads.

The older man looked up at the tree.

'You speak to anyone round here and they'll tell you about strange things they've seen or heard. Gunfire, screaming, that sort of thing. His whole life, my father always said it was nothing but silly superstition.'

Tom wasn't sure if it was the wind or the story but the hair on his arms prickled.

'Not long before he died,' Grimmond went on, 'my father said he'd dreamt of a place with a red sky. That it was always night there and it was always on fire.. Maybe they were just the ravings of a half-crazed crippled old man but they always scared the living hell out of me.'

Grimmond pulled his jacket tighter around himself.

He was a sober man Tom. Never trusted a damn thing unless he could hold it in his own hand. The way he spoke of this place, it was like he'd been there.'

'My father spoke of one other thing, this tree…as if somehow, it was linked to his dreams.'

Grimmond started to walk back to the path.

'Did you ever have any of these dreams?' asked Tom.

The big man stopped.

'Nothing like what my father described.'

He looked off into the distance.

'Days after my father passed away I came here. I don't know why. There was a man, he stood where you are now. He didn't say much, just that he liked the tree. Said it reminded him of my father. I never saw him again after that. To this day I've never felt a chill go through me like that.'

Side by side they went back down the path, towards the cars.

'What are you going to do about the tree?' asked Tom.

'Bind and seal it up, don't want any animals getting in. It'll take years for that to mend.'

Tom watched as Grimmond climbed into his car. Danny was already sitting in his transit, ready to leave.

The two cars fired up their engines and drove down the path.

Lisa appeared next to him with a cup of tea. Tom took her hand.

'I may need something a little stronger.'

<u>10</u>

The days merged as Tom slept less and less. Lisa hovered over him constantly, a worried expression on her face.

She'd tried talking to him again about that night but so far he had managed to avoid it. He spent most of his time in the workshop trying to stay awake. At night he read books and did his best not to think.

Danny and the Grimmond had been round everyday working on the tree, they were trying to rig something around the trunk involving steel bolts. It was all very noisy.

Tom sensed the man was hiding something more but he wouldn't talk in front of Danny.

A few days later, Lisa finally cornered him while he made up the dialysis machine. He was exhausted and had done something wrong. The machine started to alarm.

She came over to help.

'I think you should let me do this tonight' she said.

Tom raised his hands in defeat and moved away. Lisa continued sorting the equipment.

'I think it's time we talked,' she said with her back to him. 'The doctor said you could be going through a breakdown because of everything. I told him that was nonsense but after the last few days… I'm not so sure. You need to tell me what's going on.'

Tom sighed and wheeled over to the window. He stared out at the tree, its branches swayed in the breeze. Moonlight was glinting off the scaffolding circling the trunk; Grimmond's 'long term solution'.

'If I told you something was trying to get me while I slept, what would you say?'

She turned to face him.

'I'd say it was probably a metaphor for something else, your sub-conscience telling you things weren't right.'

'What if I told you those dreams were trying to get me when I was awake too?'

'Like you're seeing things that aren't there?' Lisa asked.

She reached over to a shoe box next to the bed, inside was all his medicines. She inspected one of the leaflets.

'Do any of these have side effects?' she asked.

Tom took the box of pills away and took her hands in his.

'This has nothing to do with the meds Lisa. Something is happening to me and I think it has to do with that tree.

Ever since we moved here I've had dreams, every one of them has had that damn tree dead centre. Lately though, it's

been different. They've gotten more…
real.'

Tom went on to tell her about the doorway and the carvings. Finally he told her about what happened in the living room that night.

Afterwards, Lisa sat in silence on the bed.

'Ok,' she said. 'I want to go and have another look at the tree. Will you come with me?'

'Of course,' said Tom, surprised 'Does this mean you believe me?'

'I need to see the writing myself before we speak any more. I only got a quick glance at it before.'

They went through to the kitchen, put on their coats and took up a couple of torches.

The snow had taken hold the night before. The whole garden had turned into a frozen tundra.

Lisa struggled to push the wheelchair through the snow. They had tried clearing it that morning but the weather swallowed the path back up within hours.

Wind battered them from every direction as they slowly moved round the house.

Snow clung to the oak tree branches, making them droop lower than usual.

Moonlight shone off the ice turning everything black and white. Grimmond's scaffolding around the tree had been engulfed by drifts.

Dark wooden tendrils arched over their heads, swaying heavily with every pass of wind.

The snow was too thick around the tree to push the chair any further. Lisa left Tom a few yards back while she waded over to the oak.

She dug a hole through the drift covering the scaffold. The crack in the trunk had been covered by a sheet of tarpaulin, a weak attempt to stop the weather getting in and rotting the inside.

Lisa tore the sheet down, behind it Tom could see the outline of the fissure.

It had gotten even wider in the last few days and was now big enough for a man to walk into. He watched as Lisa shone the torch around the edges.

'Someone's carved a frame around the crack!' shouted Lisa.

In his dreams, the doorway had an ornate frame too.

The torch strafed back and forth over the trunk. It stopped over the crack itself, but Tom couldn't make out what Lisa was focusing on.

'I think I see something else carved in the wood,' she said.

Tom looked around. Other than the wind, it was totally silent. He suddenly felt unsafe.

'Lisa, come back. I don't think we should be here.'

'Hold on' she said. 'I think it's different...'

The torch fell to the ground, its light lying dead in the snow.

'Lisa?' called Tom.

Silence.

Tom pushed the chair as far as he could onto the lawn but the wheels caught in the snow.

'Lisa!'

He flung himself out of the chair onto the snow covered ground.

Tom dragged his body towards the tree, to the spot where his wife should be.

He grabbed the fallen torch and shone it round the garden. She was nowhere to be seen.

'Lisa…!'

The torch light reflected off something metallic in the trunk of the tree.

He tried to hold the beam steady.

A hand hung limply from inside the crack, a gold wedding ring glinting in the torch light.

Tom pulled wildly at the hand, screaming his wife's name again and again.

<u>11</u>

He could feel the knots of the tree against his back, they writhed back and forth as if something was trying to claw its way out. Around him the crimson sky seemed to boil. Flames burned deep inside the dark nebulous clouds overhead.

Was he causing it? Was it even his dream anymore?

Everything around him was hazy and indistinct, ground shimmered as if he were saw from a great distance. Bracing against the great tree, Tom tried to stand but pain shot through his body. His legs lay limp and mocking on the earth in front of him.

A peal of thunder cracked somewhere off in the distance followed by a blast of searing wind.

Something moved in the haze ahead. At first it was nothing more than a flicker out in the fire-torn savannah.

'Senseless visions of a half-crazed cripple,' Grimmond's story of his father came to Tom's mind.

Something else moved off in the other direction, then another and another. Rippling images appeared and disappeared across the fields. They were getting closer.

Men, the mirages were men, hundreds of them.

Tom shouted out to the closest but his only reply was a familiar voice.

'They can't hear you.'

Standing next to him looking down was the cloaked figure from his living room. Even in broad daylight, Tom could barely make out his features.

He could see the piercing white eyes staring out from underneath the figure's cowl. Tom reached out violently to him but collapsed onto the dusty ground, gasping in pain.

'Where's is she?' rasped Tom.

The images out in the field had stopped moving.

Were they were listening to the conversation?

Some were carrying rifles, others had swords. They were all dressed the same. Cloaks covered old white shirts, leather boots with buckles. Some wore Scottish bonnets – Tam o' Shanters. Their faces were bloodied and dirty.

'Who are you?' shouted Tom.

'Names have no meaning here. I left my own behind when I first came here. So will you… by the end.'

Tom tried to make sense of what was happening around him but the pain and the heat kept clouding his mind.

'You don't have long here Tom. The time will come soon enough.'

With that a deathly silence fell, leaving Tom sprawled in the dust.

Out in the fields the figures looked on, pity written on their gaunt scarred faces.

Another roll of thunder cracked overhead, louder this time, followed by a blinding flash of lightning. Tom covered his eyes.

He awoke to the dull sounds of the dialysis machine pumping next to him.

Something was different.

The smell was all wrong, disinfectant, cleaning agents, linoleum. Clinical.

Tom opened his eyes.

The walls around him were a dull white colour, a line of sickly green paint separated the top from the bottom. Hospital.

Tom tried to sit up but a canvas belt strapped over his chest prevented it, his arms had been tied at the wrists to the metal railings along the side of the bed. His burnt hand struggled uselessly.

He could feel the panic rising in his stomach.

'It's alright Tom, don't worry' said a familiar voice beside him.

Callum Grimmond sat in a red plastic chair against the wall. A newspaper lay folded in his lap.

'What am I doing here?' demanded Tom. 'How did I get here?'

'I found you this morning outside the house. You were lying next to the oak.

In a right state you were.'

Tom struggled against his restraints.

'I can't be here... Lisa...'

'The doctors say you've got a mild case of hypothermia' continued Grimmond, 'You should be back on your feet, figuratively of course, in a few days.'

'Why am I tied up like this?'

'You weren't exactly being cooperative when they brought you in. They said it was for your own safety.'

'Grimmond, I have to get out of here… I have to save her…'

Tom stopped and looked the landlord in the face.

'You must have seen her. The hand… the tree.'

Grimmond sighed and stood up, his paper falling to the floor. He walked over and took hold of Tom's hand.

'I'm sorry Tom, I truly am.'

'No…' he cried 'she's alive… he took her so that I would follow! I have to go back… to get her…'

'Who took her?' asked Grimmond.

'Remember what your father said, about the tree and the dreams… it's all true. There's someone there, has been all along.

'Tom, you're not making any sense…'

'You've got to believe me!' cried Tom

A nurse appeared at the door. Her white uniform was a size too small for her large frame.

'What's going on here?' she said, irritation clear on her face.

'It's nothing' said Grimmond. 'He's just a bit upset at being all tied up.'

'Well if he doesn't calm down he'll be staying like that for the night.'

Tom tried to put some calm into his voice.

'Nurse, there's nothing wrong. I was just surprised that's all.'

The nurse nodded, satisfied at getting her way.

'I'll talk to the doctor, see if he's ok with the restraints coming off.'

The nurse left the room. The sound of her footsteps receding down the linoleum floored hallway.

Grimmond got up and stood in the doorway.

'I have to go' he said 'but I'll be back later to check on you. Get some rest.'

Tom tried to reach out to the man but his restraints held.

'Please… you have to help me…'

The doorway was empty except for the sound of Grimmond's footsteps echoing off in the distance.

<u>12</u>

Tom looked around the room. His wheelchair lay at the bottom of the bed. His cloths were folded on a bench against the wall.

He had to save Lisa.

Clenching his fist, the burn on his hand stung. He looked down. There was something smeared over the wound – a salve.

Tom closed his eyes and braced himself. Twisting the burnt palm he tried to get some of the oily salve onto the binding. Biting down hard Tom pulled his hand through the strap.

It was working.

His arm felt like it was on fire but it was working.

After what felt like hours, Tom sat on the end of the bed exhausted. His arm lay lifelessly next to him, the burn red and raw from the exercise.

He didn't have time to recover. Quickly unhooking himself from the dialysis machine, he pulled the wheelchair round the bed. He moved over to the wall and pulled on his clothes.

Through the window he could see the sun, like a ticking clock, it was heading towards the horizon.

The ward was quiet; he could hear nurses in the other rooms quietly talking amongst themselves. This was his only chance.

Tom wheeled himself out of the room and down the corridor, the polished floors made pushing the chair easy but every movement sent a shock of pain through his hand. He was sweating by the time he reached the exit.

Outside a thick layer of snow covered the ground. He headed towards the hospital taxi rank. It was near the entrance but there were no cars cabs in the cue.

Tom sat in the wheelchair, his arms hanging down by his side. Snow flake began to fall around him, he'd never felt more lost or alone.

Had he let Lisa down? Had he let her down in a way she never would have?

'Tom!' shouted a voice

He looked up. A white transit van had pulled up alongside him. Danny's face peered out the window.

13

'What are you doing here?' asked Tom.

Danny had heaved Tom into the back of the van. He was now driving through the snow storm back to the house.

'Mr Grimmond told me to get down here' said the young man. 'Asked me to make sure you were comfortable. I didn't think he meant this.'

Danny was peering through the windscreen of the van. He could only see a few feet in front of them.

'You're not looking that great.'

Tom looked himself up and down. His shirt was torn where he'd ripped off a scrap for his burnt hand and his jeans were covered in mud from where he lay in the garden.

'Where's Grimmond?' said Tom.

'He's waiting at your place. Said he wanted to make sure everything was ok'

Tom felt a flicker of hope.

'Did he say anything to you? Anything about my wife?'

'No' replied Danny 'but he was busy round that old oak tree the whole time. First time I've ever hear him talk about getting rid of it.'

'What do you mean?' said Tom.

'He said it was too dangerous, that he should get rid of it for good.'

Tom's hope turned to horror.

'He can't… It could be the only way to get her back…'

'Get who back?'

'We have to get back to the house Danny, as quickly as we can.'

'We're going as fast as we can Tom' said Danny angrily 'any faster and we may end up in a ditch.'

Tom felt the van begin to spin around him.

'Maybe you should tell me what's going on?'

Realising he may have found an ally, Tom told him everything, from the dreams to the tree to Lisa's disappearance.

Danny didn't look like he believed much of it but at least he made the van go a little faster.

It took the best part of an hour to reach the house. By then the storm had let up and it was dark.

From inside the van Tom could see the silhouette of the tree behind the house, its spidery branches glowing with a thin layer of snow.

The house was dark, bar a single light coming from the kitchen window.

'Can you see him?' asked Tom.

'Hang on, I'll go see.'

He stepped out of the van and turned to Tom.

'Do you want a hand getting into the house first?'

'No, just help me out.'

Danny lifted him out of the van and into the waiting chair.

The cold wind bit through his clothes like a wild animal. Tom pulled his hood up in a futile attempt to stave of hypothermia.

Danny trudged off in the direction of the house, Tom following behind him.

He watched as Danny knocked at the door and got no answer. He pulled the handle and went in, his shadow passing in front of the kitchen window.

Tom turned the wheelchair around, pushing himself down into the frozen garden.

Somewhere a fire was burning. The smell hung in the wind. Then he heard it, a faint crackling sound.

A sudden fear ran though him.

'Danny!' he shouted.

No answer.

He made his way across the garden. A ruddy glow was flickering to life from round the corner.

'NO!' shouted Tom.

As he rounded the bend Tom stopped and stared at the huge oak.

Gouts of flame leapt from branch to branch, snaking into every notch and crevice. The bark had begun to shrivel and crack in the heat. Great plumes of smoke were rising to the sky blotting out the moon. The seething flames gave the only light now.

In front of the oak stood a silhouette, its arms hanging limply by its side. Its shoulders were slumped, shaking, crying.

'STOP! PLEASE!' screamed Tom.

The head turned slowly towards Tom.

Callum Grimmond's face was dark from soot and smoke. Flames reflected back at Tom from the landlord's tear-stricken eyes.

'What have you done?' screamed Tom.

He moved the wheelchair over the melting snow.

He stopped in front of Grimmond, looking him in the eye.

'WHAT HAVE YOU DONE?'

'He had to be stopped…' Grimmond spoke quietly.

Tom pushed past the big man towards the tree.

Like an open furnace the heat hit him. The air in his lungs burnt away leaving him gasping for breath.

He looked up at the oak, the trunk had all but split in two, great rungs of fire raced up either side. In the centre there was nothing but darkness, untouched by the flames it could have been the gateway to hell itself.

The roar from the blaze sounded like a thousand screams.

'Lisa,' he rasped.

Could he hear her in amongst it all? Was she screaming for him?

Behind him Grimmond continued to sob.

'They're all gone… he took them… I didn't believe. I should have believed.'

Tom looked around him.

Shadows danced around the two men. The crackles from the fire turned to gunshots, and the screams of the dying surrounded him. Men with rifles cowered on the ground, some clutched crosses to their chest.

A man crouched close to Tom, a small knife clutched in his hand. Tears streaked his face as he muttered a prayer. From somewhere, a shot erupted. Tom watched as the praying man was thrown backward. Smoke drifted from his forehead.

Under the tree Tom spotted a single man, dressed similarly to the others on the field. He wore a malicious grin. He knew he was safe. A traitor.

The shadows around Tom began to disappear. The sky overhead had turned red from the fire of the tree.

'It was such a long time ago,' said a voice by his shoulder.

Tom turned expecting to see Grimmond, but knew somehow that it would be the familiar stranger from his dreams standing next to him.

'I was told nobody would die,' he continued. 'They would become prisoners of war.'

The dusty voice spoke without emotion, as if recounting someone else's story.

'You betrayed them,' Tom said.

'Yes. I was left alive. They weren't.

The next day I was bound to this tree, proclaimed a coward and a traitor and shot in the legs. I died here.'

'I had a life!' cried Tom

'So did I. A wife, a family. They were all taken from me. Who was there to protect me Tom? All I wanted was to get back to them alive.'

Tom watched as the figure moved over to the tree.

'In death I waited for them to come and find me. To take me home, but no one came. I was forgotten. My bones left to rot.'

Tom could almost see the stranger's body withered and crumbled into the ground.

'You were a traitor.'

'And this is my punishment. For three hundred years I have been trapped here amidst flame and fire. Tied to this infernal tree. What was I to do but take my revenge?'

'Why me?' asked Tom quietly. 'Why Lisa?'

The figure turned back to him.

'Your fate is not sealed yet Tom. You have a choice. A choice I never had.'

Tom looked up.

'Save her… Save Lisa,' he said.

The figure's lips peeled back into a smile.

'There's always a price Tom. Are you willing to pay it?'

'Please, just let her go.'

<u>14</u>

Tom lay on his back. The sun was up. Pristine white clouds dotted a sapphire blue sky above his head. He could hear birds singing somewhere in the distance.

Confused, he sat up.

He was back behind the house. Beside him, the twisted and charred remains of the tree sat silently. The burnt-out hollow of the trunk had collapsed in on itself. A gust of wind turned blew dead earth around him. Dry leaves and twigs circled his feet before being taken off in another direction.

From around the corner, Tom heard the sound of laughing.

He walked back along the garden path to see a small unfamiliar car parked in the driveway. From the front seat, a man held out an ice cream to a little ponytailed girl running up to him.

The car's ignition turned, and the engine churned to life. A puff of smoke burst from the exhaust. The man behind the wheel called out.

'Come on sweety. Time to go!'

'Alright, I'm coming,' shouted a familiar voice.

Tom felt a surge of joy.

He heard her light footsteps running over the gravel path towards the car. She stopped and looked out at the mountains ahead, her orange silk scarf blowing in the breeze.

Tom started running towards the car. He screamed Lisa's name over and over, but she couldn't hear him. He ran behind the car for as long as he could, then fell to his knees as it disappeared out of view.

'What did you do?' he sobbed.

'There's always a price to pay,' whispered the voice.

Tom looked up through the tears.

'I had a life,' he cried.

'So did I.'

He turned to the house, seeing it for the first time. It was a crumbling ruin, unloved and unlived in for hundreds of years.

Tom collapsed backward, as the world began to spin.

The red sky above burned brightly over his head.

He was alone.

COLD FRONT

There's a bogle by the bour-tree
at the lang loan heid,
I canna thole the thoucht o'him,
he fills ma he'rt wi' dreid,
He skirls like a hoolet,
an' he rattles a' his banes,
An gi'es himsel' an unco fash
to fricht wee weans.

He's never there by daylicht,
but ance the gloamin' fa's
He creeps alang the heid-rig,
an through the tattie-shaws
Syne splairges through the burn
An' comes sprachlin ower the stanes,
Then coories doun ahint the dyke
to fricht wee weans.

I canna say I've seen him,
an' it's no that I am blin',
But, whene'er I pass the bour-tree,
I steek ma een an' rin.
An' though I get a tum'le whiles
I'd rather thole sic pains,
Than look upon the likes o' yon
that frichts wee weans.

1

They'd been sitting on the bus for hours. The traffic had slowed to a crawl somewhere outside of Perth and hadn't gotten any better.

Katie stared outside the double-glazed bus window. Rain pelted off the bonnets of the cars below. Dark forests nestled close to the road on either side of them blocking out whatever light the rain let in. She looked across the seat at Laura who had dozed off.

Katie smiled and picked up the carton of juice, putting it in the bag hanging off the armrest.

Their plan was to go up to Pitlochry for a long weekend. Things had been hectic the last few months and she felt she needed the break.

Laura had wanted to go abroad. 'Some fun in the sun,' she had said with a wink.

That was the last thing Katie was interested in. She just wanted to relax and forget about everything for a couple of days.

She'd argued for Pitlochry; it wasn't too far away from the city. It was where her family used to go for holidays when she was young.

She remembered camping there for two weeks every year, on the banks of Loch Tummel.

The five of them would squeeze into the tent at night and listen as Mum told stories about Scotland of old. Dad would sit outside smoking his pipe listening to 60's music, only coming in when the midges were unbearable.

They'd wake to the smell of a gas stove. First order of business, a cup of tea. They all had their own camping cups, stained from years of use. Then came the smell of bacon frying in the open air.

She couldn't think what they did during the day - maybe the occasional day-trip, but mostly they went into Pitlochry town centre to play on the arcades. The rest of the time was spent at the campsite, playing around outside with her brothers.

Laura stirred suddenly, her eyes fluttered open. She took one look outside and swore under her breath before turning and going back to sleep.

Outside, a disused building lot passed by. It used to be a café. Dad would stop there on the way back from a trip to get them fish and chips for lunch, followed by jelly and ice-cream. The jelly was shaped like a dinosaur.

Katie wondered if her brothers ever missed it. She rarely spoke with them. They had their own families to tend to now.

2

The bus dropped them off two hours late. It was almost dark but at least the rain had stopped. Next to them a large white building sat silently. A sign hanging from the side of the door announced it as 'The Ferryman's Hotel and Pub'. Either side, small shops lined the single high street. Nothing was open.

'Looks like everything's closed up for the night,' said Katie.

'Or the decade,' added Laura.

'If we can get a taxi we'll be fine, I think,' replied Katie.

Laura pulled out her phone, sighed and held it up for Katie to see.

'No reception.'

'I'll go in and use the payphone,' said Katie walking towards the hotel.

110

'Hope you got your banjo handy,' smirked Laura.

Inside was dark and musty. The low-beamed ceiling made her want to stoop. There was nobody at reception but there was a quiet murmur coming from a room down the hall. The soft clinking of glasses mixed with muted voices told her it was the pub section of the hotel.

'Can I help?' came a woman's voice.

Katie turned to see a head poking out a room next to reception, long brown hair falling down past the shoulders.

'Um…yes, do you have a payphone and maybe the number of a local taxi firm?'

'Aye of course. Come on over.'

The woman shuffled out of the door. Her hands stretching out in front of her, she made her way towards the desk.

It was only then Katie noticed the milky white of the woman's eyes. She was blind.

'Oh, welcome to The Ferryman. I'm Moira.'

Moira wore a long dress under a baggy cardigan that accentuated her skinny frame. She rummaged about the desk looking for something.

'The phone's through in the pub but if you give me a minute, I'll find you the taxi number. It's quiet in the town tonight so Jim should only be a few minutes.'

'Jim?'

'The taxi,' Moira laughed. 'Off you go now, the pub's just ahead of you. You'll see the phone on the left.'

The pub down the hall was smaller than expected, just five or six small tables situated around a horseshoe bar. A television on the wall flickered with static. There were only a few people in. Regulars, she guessed. They stopped what they were doing and smiled as she walked in.

An old woman sat alone at the bar with a newspaper and nip of whiskey. Across from her a couple stood next to a fruit machine, its neon lights reflecting off their faces.

Katie nodded to each in turn as she made her way towards the phone.

After a few minutes Moira came into the room.

'Anybody got Jim's number? I'm having trouble seeing it.'

The three patrons laughed at her joke.

'No need for that!' shouted a voice from the doorway.

A large bearded man stood looking at her. He wore a flat cap and his cheeks were the colour of beetroot.

'Ahh Jim!' said Moira 'We were just in need of your services.'

'Of course you were,' bellowed the big man.

He strode across the room towards her, his heavy footsteps shaking the planks beneath their feet.

'Where you going lass? Big Jim'll get you there. Nae worries.'

Katie felt her eyes water as his breath wafted over. Big Jim clearly liked a drink.

'To the Ardgualich campsite? It's by the loch.'

The woman by the bar looked up.

'That's my place dear.' she said closing her paper. 'The bus is always late. Thought you might need a wee lift. I'm Mary.

She turned to Big Jim.

'You'll give us a hand with the lassie's bags eh Jim?'

'Well seeing as you cheated me out of a fare…' he winked at Katie then turned to the bar.

'MOIRA! Whisky to go. Cheers lass.'

Katie watched as the blind woman passed him a waiting glass. He raised it to his lips and downed it in one.

'Right' he said slamming the glass onto the bar. 'Ready to go?'

They walked back through the reception where Katie noticed for the first time, something odd behind the desk. Pinned across a board were pictures of girls, beneath each picture the word 'MISSING' in bold print.

'What happened to all these women?'

'Och that's old stuff' replied Mary, moving towards the door. 'If Moira could see them,

115

she'd maybe remember to take them down.'

Katie followed behind the woman. Outside, Laura was leaning against the wall. Big Jim was already there, looking her up and down. 'You needin' a taxi love?'

Laura looked over at Katie, one eyebrow arched.

'*Really*?'

'She's with me. Laura, this is Mary. She owns the site we're going to. She came to pick us up.'

Jim pushed himself away from the wall and towards an old 4x4 parked by the pavement.

He wrenched open the rear passenger door.

'Your chariot m'ladies.'

Mary got in behind the wheel and started the engine. Big Jim was still bowing floridly at them from the pavement as they sped off.

***

Mary fiddled with the dials on the dashboard until a burst of static erupted through the car. They could hear a faint voice through the crackle.

"It'll be a dry night with a cold front coming up from the south. We expect a clear, bright night leading to a light shower that should blow off by morning…"

The rest of the report was lost to static.

'Sounds like you'll have a nice clear night to pitch up'.

They soon left behind the farmland and were driving through thick forest. The tell-tale sparkle of water glinted through the trees. In front of them, a huge building reared out of nowhere, its turrets silhouetted against the setting sun.

'I don't remember this,' said Katie.

'That's the Laird's estate,' said Mary.

Katie waited for her to say more but she just sped past the large wrought iron gates without another word.

She watched the forest swallow the building back up as they drove away.

The road suddenly turned off into the forest and up a steep hill leaving the loch behind them. Trees flickered past the window until there was nothing to see but the dark undergrowth in between.

Mary glanced across at Katie.

'Have you stayed with us before dear?'

'Not for a long time. My family used to come here years ago. Tom and Eve?'

'Oh aye. Now I remember.' Smiled Mary 'I've no' seen them in years. How they getting on?'

Katie swallowed.

'They passed away last month. They loved this place.'

'Och! I'm sorry dear. I shouldn't have opened ma big mouth...'

'No, it's fine. Honestly. It's nice to come up... relive some old memories.'

Mary nodded.

'I can still see you as a wee girl. You haven't really changed.'

Eventually they pulled up to an old wooden gate -'Ardgualich Camping and Caravanning site'.

The path down to the site was muddy and the midges had already begun to gather in clouds, but below them the splendid view of the campsite spread out in the evening glow.

It stuck out into the loch itself, and stretched beneath a sway of emerald green grass to where a copse of trees topped a small hill. A dozen caravans sat contently overlooking the water, dim lights glowing from inside their plastic windows.

On the other side, moored boats bobbed gently in the ebbing tide. In the centre stood a small farm house, smoke wisping from the chimney to join the few scattered clouds in the sky. Reflected in the still calm of Loch Tummel, the mountains soared towards the sky.

'Alright' said Laura, patting Katie on the shoulder. 'I'll accept it.'

<u>3</u>

They pitched their tent down by the water's edge, by a grassy hill out of the wind.

While Laura busied herself getting the stove ready for cooking, Katie sat down with a cup of tea and watched the sun set.

Across the way she could see the castle they drove past. Its massive walls jutted out of the forest and over the loch. Tiny lights flickered to life from unseen windows.

'You know, this is actually quite relaxing. Who knew?' said Laura sitting down next to her.

She leaned back on the grass and sighed.

Laura took out her phone and took a picture of them both.

'For posterity's sake. Nobody will believe you got me up here otherwise.'

Katie laughed.

'Ok, I can tell you're aching to break out the booze. Make mine a G&T.'

'Coming right up!'

Around the site, people had started to light up small outdoor grills, the scent drifting across the grass to them. When the last of the light disappeared the girls climbed into the tent and hunkered down to sleep. Outside, the temperature dropped and the mist began to roll in.

Katie sat up suddenly. Something made a sound outside.

She nudged Laura but she was sound asleep.

Unzipping the door, she flicked on the torch. The loch was shrouded in a fog, its thick tendrils threatening to invade the tent. She crawled out, closing the flap behind her.

The mist swirled about Katie's feet. Somewhere, a horn blew softly. Out across water, the muted lights of the castle glowed sullenly.

Suddenly, a flash of light ignited across the fog with a ruddy yellow colour, like a naked flame. It seemed to be coming from the castle. She could see the dark hulk of the walls outlined against the light.

Somewhere, someone was singing. She listened closely, trying to pick up the words.

> *He's never there by daylicht,*
> *but ance the cloamin' fa's...*

A gust of wind took away the rest of the words.

Katie shivered in spite of herself.

Something about the line sparked a memory, but like a dream it slipped out of her reach the harder she tried to remember it.

The mist began to grow thin, retreating back towards the centre of the loch. It was later than she thought. Over the mountains the first slivers of sunlight were beginning to show. Feeling the chill, she climbed back into the tent.

She woke to the smell of the gas stove and the sound of boiling water. Laura was sitting down by the loch's edge, skimming stones.

'Morning,' yawned Katie. 'You're up early?'

'Speak for yourself,' she replied.

Katie looked at her watch. It was nearly eleven o'clock. She watched as one of Laura's skimmers bounced out into the surf.

'I remember being a lot better at this' she said with her back still turned. 'My dad and I used to go to this wee place in the Lake District. We'd stay there for a couple of weeks in a rented cottage. He liked to fish…'

Laura went silent.

Katie poured them both a cup of tea and brought it over.

She told Laura about the fog and the lights in the mist.

'Creepy. Maybe they were having a party?'

'Who knows? All the way out here, people can do a lot and get away with it.'

After a healthy helping of bacon and eggs, Katie pulled out a book and sat by the Loch. Laura managed a full thirty minutes of sitting restlessly before suggesting they take a walk.

They set off through a dense thicket of ferns alongside the jetty. Laura grabbed a tall stick off the ground and called it her staff.

The path ran down by the edge of the loch and through the forest. Pretty soon they were surrounded by ancient oaks and pinewood. The path was far smaller than Katie remembered. In places it was little more than an animal track.

By lunch they were exhausted, scratched, dirty and not getting along. Laura's staff had quickly become an annoying necessity primarily for whacking aside branches and as a dip stick for various mud pools.

Laura suddenly flung the stick to the ground.

'I can't believe this is how you wanted to spend the weekend!'

She took a few steps forward and tripped over a large root.

'We could have been anywhere. But no, you wanted to relive your bloody childhood camping trip!'

'Come on,' placated Katie. 'If we head up the way, we come out at the road.'

'Oh goodie' said Laura grabbing her stick from the ground and walking on.

Her first step sunk into a mud patch, her fancy trainers leaving a distinctive swoosh mark in the brown muck.

'I hate this place.'

She grabbed a stone off the ground and threw it in frustration. It disappeared into a bush, landing with a clang. Laura climbed over and shoved her stick through the leaves. It hit something metallic.

She pushed aside the bush to reveal a large black iron fence. It was encased in an old stone dyke build into the ground.

'Finally! Civilization!'

Katie could see the railing reached right through the forest, blocking their path.

The other side was made up of more forest, but behind it though rose moss covered stones of a wall. The castle.

Overhead a bird squawked. She suddenly felt cold. The air around them had turned stale; there wasn't a breath of wind.

'I thought we'd come farther than this' said Laura. 'We've been walking for hours.'

A small arched gate was built into the rock. Its hinges were orange with rust. Dead leaves and branches had gathered a foot deep at the bottom.

Laura began to open it.

'Wait!' said Katie quietly 'What if they think we're trespassing?'

She didn't want Laura to know she was scared. Something about the other side of the fence made her feel uneasy.

'Then we're trespassing,' replied Laura, 'We'll go in, find the driveway and walk

128

up to the road. That's all. They can't get pissed about that.'

It was who 'they' were that worried Katie.

The old iron screeched in protest as they pushed the gate open. Flakes of rust floated down to join the leaves and branches scattered at the bottom.

Even though Katie still felt a chill in the air, Laura took off her jacket.

She could see beads of sweat on Laura's forehead.

In the distance, the castle walls loomed dark and silent. Years of moss and algae made the stone look diseased. At its highest, the building dwarfed the nearest trees, and everything else around it. Ancient arrow slits looked down on them like eyes as they walked.

Laura had wandered ahead. Arms hanging limply by her side, the staff lay discarded on the ground behind her.

'You alright?' asked Katie, retrieving the stick.

Laura continued walking.

'Hey!'

She ran up and grabbed her by the shoulder. Her skin was clammy with sweat.

'Hey, you listening?'

Laura stopped and looked around, as if coming out of a trance. She turned and looked at Katie.

'Sorry… I don't know what happened… it was like I seeing and hearing everything through a haze.'

'You feeling alright now?' asked Katie.

'I think so. I could do with a drink of water though.'

As if on cue, they heard the sound of rushing water coming from somewhere ahead of them. Laura moved towards the noise.

She saw the spray from the falls first.

'Oh my' said Laura running towards it.

She was down on her knees scooping handfuls of the water into her mouth before Katie could stop her.

The cool, clear liquid cascaded down and into a natural well. Round pebbles lay at the bottom of the pool, the sun catching their shade and shape perfectly.

Katie wasn't sure if she'd ever saw anything so perfect in her life.

She dipped a quivering hand into the cool water and was about to raise it to her lips when yet again she felt the chill ripple through her body. Something was wrong.

She looked again at the pool, noticing for the first time the waves of red muddying it. Her eyes followed the red to behind the falls where something lay. A long white dress trailed into the water. Milky pale arms floated lifelessly in the current while a mass of brown curls cascaded limply from the top of the dress. A trail of blood flowed from underneath the remains.

'Stop!' screamed Katie

She pulled Laura away.

'Look! There's a body in the water!'

Her friend stared at her as if she'd gone mad.

'What are you talking about?!'

Katie pointed again. But it was gone. A patch of moss covered a stone in its place.

'But I was sure I saw...'

Laura shook her head.

'What's going on with you? Come on.'

They wound through the trees round to the front of the castle and at last, a driveway leading back to the road.

A sound drifted through the silence. It was the same voices from the night before. Like a choir they rose in harmony, their song blowing through the trees.

... bogle by the bour-tree at the lang loan heid...

It was then Katie realised that Laura wasn't beside her. Instead standing stock-still in front of the castle doors, which were ten foot tall and studded with black metal bolts.

Even though it was noticeably colder than earlier, Laura's jacket was still off and she was visibly sweating. Her eyes were closed and she was swaying on the balls of her feet.

'LAURA!'

Katie ran back down to her. She was tired and wanted nothing more than to get back to the tent.

'What are you doing? Come on.'.

Laura's eyes rolled back and a dreamy smile crept across her face.

'Can you not hear it?' She whispered 'They're singing to us.'

Katie stepped back.

She took Laura's arm and tried to move her away.

'Come on Laura! PLEASE!'

'No!' she said wresting her arm away. 'It's beautiful, I want to listen to them.'

From behind, Katie heard the clank of bolts and creaking wood. The great door had begun to open. A crack down the centre started to widen, the darkness beyond swallowing the light.

To her horror, Laura took a step into that darkness.

Katie grabbed her friend by the arm again.

Laura screamed in her face. Her hands reached up to as if to scratch her. Dust from the gravel driveway kicked up around them. Behind, the doors of the castle had silently swung closed.

Laura's struggling grew weaker and weaker the closer to the gate they got until finally she slumped on the ground, exhausted.

Laura, wake up.'

Her eyes fluttered open. She had tears in her eyes.

'What's wrong?' she mumbled, 'Are we back at the tent?'

'No, not yet. What happened back there?'

'What do you mean?'

135

'You went nuts back there! I was really scared.'

'Sorry, I really don't know what you mean,' she said getting to her feet.

Katie looked at her aghast.

'You really don't remember?'

Laura shook her head, dusting bits of gravel off her jeans.

'Nope, but I am starving. Let's see how quickly we can get back.'

Katie stared at her back as she pushed at the massive gate, walked out onto the road and started back towards the campsite.

4

They sat quietly in front of the barbecue. The steaks they'd bought from the site shop sent up a plume of sweet smelling smoke. Katie took a sip from her glass and stared at Laura. She hadn't said a word the whole way back. Now she sat there holding her staff, prodding the meat on the grill. She seemed to be back to her usual self.

'It really is beautiful here' she said 'we should do it more often.'

Katie laughed.

'Never thought I'd hear *you* say that!'

'Hey! People can change can't they?'

A gust of wind sent the smoke billowing over them, sending them coughing. They started to laugh.

To Katie, this was perfect. The last rays reflected off the loch, bathing them in gentle heat.

Later, after they'd eaten, Laura flicked stones into the water while humming a song.

'What is that?' asked Katie.

'What is what?'

'That song?'

'I don't know. Must've heard it somewhere though. I can't get it out of my head.'

'Around this time,' said Katie, glancing towards the castle, 'Mum would always tell us a story. You know, to round off the day. Sometimes it would be an old fairy tale other days it would be something to do with Scotland. Occasionally Dad would make a bonfire and we'd make up our own stories over it.'

Laura stared across the water.

'We never did that. Our mum preferred to dump us at whatever cabaret the resort had on that night. Then she'd go off to the casino.'

She threw another rock into the loch.

'Sometimes I think my dad wouldn't have minded things a little bit more natural. Camping, stories. Normal family life. That was never going to happen while they were together though. You should've heard what mum said when I told her our plans for this weekend. I swear she was disgusted at me.'

A heavy silence hung in the air.

Laura started humming again.

Katie turned when she heard the sound of footsteps on the gravel next to them. It was Mary, holding a sheet of paper in her hand.

'Hi there. Just a quick visit, thought you might want to see this.'

She handed the sheet to Katie. It was an old photograph of the site. A younger Mary stood in the centre of a group of people. In the front sat three children. Next to them were her parents.

'I remember this!' cried Katie, 'I can't believe you kept it all this time.'

Mary smiled.

'To tell the truth I only found it the other day. It was sitting in amongst a pile of old receipts. I thought you might like it?'

Katie felt her eyes well up.

'Thank you. Thank you so much!'

She got up and hugged the old woman.

That night Laura went to bed early saying she had a headache. Katie stayed out with a lantern looking at the photo.

***

Laura twisted and turned in her sleeping bag. She kept mumbling how hot it was. Several times Katie had to physically stop her climbing out of the bag.

'It's freezing Laura,' she tried whispering to her. 'I'll get you some water, but stay wrapped up.'

Outside the fog had swept in blanketing the site again.

She crept down to the shore, cup in hand. The water was icy cold as her fingers brushed the surface of the loch.

It rippled through the fog, clear one minute, hazy the next. Katie looked up. Again the lights swirled around the shadow of the castle. It should have been a beautiful sight to behold. Instead Katie felt nothing but fear. The song seemed to float across the water and through the site. She knew those words.

Images of the campfire and her family came to mind. Her mum was reading them a poem, in Old Scots...

A cold breeze suddenly washed over her from the loch. Shivering, Katie went back inside the tent, where Laura had settled down, a strange smile across her lips as she slept.

The morning dawned cool and clear over the water. Katie opened her eyes and saw immediately that something was wrong. Laura's skin was pallid and clammy and she was shaking.

Katie kicked out of her sleeping bag.

'Laura? Are you alright?'

'My head hurts… it's so hot.'

Katie got up.

'Hang on, I'll go check up at the house and see if Mary has any painkillers.'

She walked up through the site and knocked on the front door of the farmhouse.

Mary opened the door. She was already dressed.

'Oh hello dear. What can I do for you?'

'I'm sorry to bother you Mary but do have any aspirin? Laura's unwell.'

The old woman shook her head.

'I'm sorry, I've none. There must be something goin' about this morning. You're the fourth to ask today.'

Katie nodded her thanks. She wasn't sure what to do.

'Look' said Mary catching her by the arm. 'I've to go into town anyway. Why don't you come with me and you can pick up some there. We'll be back within the hour.'

'Ok, yeah that would be great. Thanks. I'll go and grab my bag.'

Back at the tent, she found Laura sitting next to the loch. Droplets of sweat ran down her brow.

'Mary's going to drive me into town. I'll be back as soon as I can ok?'

Laura nodded, the dreamy smile still crossing her features.

'Take your time. It really is beautiful here.'

She started humming again.

***

Mary's 4x4 drove along winding road back to Pitlochry.

The car slowed as it turned a tight corner. On Katie's right, the wrought iron gates of the castle came into view.

A shiver ran up her spine at the memory of the place.

'Have you ever met the Laird?' she asked pointing.

Mary gave the gates a dark look.

'I don't think anybody has, dear. The place is shut up tight most of the time. I'll tell you this though. Ever since it's been back in use there's been some strange goings-on.'

'Like the lights?' asked Katie.

The castle walls disappeared into the woods behind them.

'Aye,' said Mary quietly, 'The lights. Or worse.'

She sat up behind the wheel suddenly.

'Don't listen to me lass, just a wee bit of superstition, that's all. It gets the better of all of us sometimes.

They drove the rest of the way in silence.

Mary dropped Katie off outside the hotel.

'I'll see you back here in twenty minutes, ok?'

145

Without waiting for a reply the vehicle sped off down the street.

Pitlochry was quite different in the daytime. The high street was packed full of day trippers, colourful backpacks bearing foreign names bobbed up and down the length of the town. The shops were open and doing brisk business. Most were selling souvenirs but a few artisan shops advertised local art and curios for those willing to pay a price.

Katie wandered into a newsagent and bought a couple of packs of Ibuprofen.

With fifteen minutes left to meet Mary, she made her way over to the hotel.
Inside, Moira was busy moving piles of paper from one side of the front desk to the other. She must have heard her come in.

'Hello there. Welcome to the Ferryman Hotel.'

'Hi there,' signalled Katie, 'I was in the other night, for the taxi?'

'Oh aye. How's it going? You having a nice time up at the site?'

'Yes it's lovely. Mary's just dropped me off to get some supplies.'

Katie looked at the board behind Moira again.

'Do you know what happened to those girls?' asked Katie Moira.

'No one knows lass,' came a voice from behind them.

Big Jim walked up next to her. He still reeked of booze but seemed steadier on his feet.

'It's a sorry business is that,' he continued. 'I dropped off some of them myself. None from round here and none of them about for more than a couple of nights before they disappeared.'

Moira crossed her chest and muttered something under her breath.

'Bogle' she whispered.

Katie thought back to the line in the poem.

'Wheesht Moira!' 'Don't mind her lass. Superstition can be an awful thing in a small place like Pitlochry.'

'What's …Bogle?' asked Katie.

'Just an old tale. Dinnae pay no mind lass.'

Jim nodded to her and walked off in the direction of the bar. She turned back to Moira but she'd also vanished back into her room.

Outside, Mary was waiting by the kerb. She honked the car's horn to signal her.

As they set off out of the village, Katie turned to her.

'What's the Bogle?'

148

'The Bogle? Who's been speaking that nonsense?'

'Moira mentioned it.'

'Moira's had a rough time of it. Gets a little excited sometimes.'

'Jim told me something similar. What's the tale though? I've never heard of it.'

'It really is so silly.' said Mary exhaling loudly. 'Apparently, in the last century, there was an old laird who fell in love with a younger woman. He gave her everything. All he wanted was to hear her sing. After several years, the woman became bored of the old laird and left him in the middle of the night, taking all his belongings and leaving nothing but a note. Before locking himself away in his keep, he issued a note to the surrounding villages. If they should ever see his wife again, they were top bring her back to him. At any cost. Nobody saw him again after that. His name was Laird Bogle.'

'That's it?'

'Aye, we grew up hearing about it. Our mothers would scare us with it if we did something bad.'

'What do you think about all the missing girls?'

'I don't know. Some probably went swimming in the loch, got taken away with the current. The police have no idea. Nobody's found any bodies so they're probably runaways.'

'What about their friends, family?'

Mary shrugged her shoulders. She stared straight ahead at the road in front. Her fists tightened on the steering wheel.

As they drove towards the loch, a thick fog descended over the road.

Mary swore under her breath as she switched the car headlights onto full beam.

'The Loch brings the weather down at the drop of a hat sometimes.'

'I remember,' joked Katie. 'More than once we'd spend the day shacking up inside the tent during storms. My dad would be the one crawling around in the rain trying to hammer tent pegs back into the ground.'

The fog grew thicker till they could see no more than five feet ahead of the bonnet. At the campsite the car slowly bumped its way down the dirt path and Katie got out and thanked Mary for the lift.

She made her way down through the fog, which hung over the pitch like a wet blanket. She stumbled when her foot tripped over something in the grass. It was one of their camping cups. Beside it was a plate. They looked like they'd just been thrown out. She saw something resembling her jumper hanging over a bush in the distance.

'Laura?' she called.

No answer.

The tent was open, all their food and drink was strewn across the front porch and more of their clothes had been dumped on the grass. The sleeping section had been ransacked, their rucksacks torn to shreds, and the sleeping bags thrown in the corner. Katie turned and felt her way down to the Loch. Laura was nowhere to be seen.

'Laura!' she shouted again.

Again, nothing.

Out of the mist one of the static caravans emerged. She went up to the door and knocked. The door swung open silently. Inside was much the same as their tent. Rubbish lay everywhere as if the occupants had just picked up and gone. She ran up to the next caravan and the next. All in disarray, all completely empty. Katie's heart pounded as she ran over to the farmhouse. The door stood open. She found Mary sitting inside, a ledger laying on her lap.

'They're all gone!' she shouted.

Mary looked up in surprise.

'Who's all gone dear?'

'Laura… the other campers. They're all gone. Everyone's gone!'

Mary stood up and walked past her out the door. She disappeared into the mist. Katie raced after her.

She could hear Mary shouting names into the fog. Katie couldn't tell where the old woman was, but her voice echoed across the site.

'Mary!'

A shadow flitted through the fog next to her.

'Mary?'

Out of the silence came a familiar voice.

Laura. She was singing.

'Laura? Is that you?'

Then the voice deepened but the song was the same.

Within seconds, it changed again to a chorus of voices.

I canna thole the thoucht o'him,
he fills ma he'rt wi' dreid,
He skirls like a hoolet, an' he rattles a' his banes,

A hand, chilly as ice, grabbed Katie's wrist. She turned quickly, it was Mary.

'We need to go.'

She pulled her through the fog to the car.

'Quick, get in.

Katie did as she was told.

Mary sat holding the steering wheel, breathing heavily. Outside, the mist eddied around the car.

'Can you hear that? asked Mary. 'The song?'

'Yes… what is it? I've heard it coming over the loch the last couple of nights too.'

Mary stiffened in the seat.

'*It's him.*'

She started the engine.

'Who?' asked Katie, her voice faltering now, as images of all the missing girls suddenly flooded her mind. 'Who's taken them…?'

Her heart seemed to pound so loudly that she could barely hear over it as Mary said,

'We have to go.'

'We can't! I have to find Laura…and the others. We have to help them!'

But Mary just wretched the car into gear. The tires dug into the soft earth till, like a catapult, the wheels broke free.

Through the fog they raced, driving along the road at break-neck pace. The bends came at them in double quick time. More than once Katie was thrown forward as Mary braked hard to stop them from going into the tree.

'Mary' shouted Katie over the roar of the engine 'please, tell me what's going on!'

Mary eased up on the accelerator; the car should have slowed down, but only seemed to speed up.

Suddenly the car lurched and the forest rose up out of the fog. At full speed, the car hit something and flipped over. Katie felt her body leave the seat and a sharp pain as she hit the roof of the car. Daggers of windscreen shards seemed to come from everywhere. The car was still moving when she felt herself, limp and weightless, flung through crumpling metal and glass.

Somewhere a flock of birds took off as one. Their wings flapped manically. Katie tried opening her eyes but only one managed the job. The other felt swollen, possibly bleeding.

The forest floor had found its way into the cab of the car. A thin layer of leaves and dirt covered the dashboard; broken branches and splinters lay where there used to be a steering wheel.

Katie couldn't tell if it was the fog clouding her mind or the crash. All her senses were muted and slow. She fumbled for a hand hold but grasped only air. She summoned as much energy as she was able to, and reached out again. Her hand caught hold of cold metal. Gripping hard she pulled herself towards it. Pushing with her legs, she found herself lying in the dirt next to the car. It lay on its side, wrapped around a tree trunk. One wheel was gone completely, and the others were buckled and bent. Steam drifted from the engine block to join the surrounding mists.

Katie lay on the forest floor. Slowly she checked her body to see if there were any injuries. Remarkably, apart from her eye and a nasty cut down the side of her leg, everything was in working order.

Once on her feet, she walked round to the other side of the car, balancing herself on the tree buried halfway through the fuselage. She felt her foot fall on something other than dirt. It was a hand. Bloodied and broken. Staring out from between the wreck of metal and wood were Mary's glassy eyes.

Katie fell back as the air seemed to leave her lungs in a rush. Ragged sobs ratcheted out of her mouth from between scratched fingers. Panicked, she tried pulling herself up but her foot slipped and she fell hard,

knocking her head against the base of a
tree. Slowly the world faded to black.

5

She was back by the loch. The aroma of trout on a fire, bought fresh from the village that day, made her mouth water. Peter and Billy were playing football behind the tent. Somewhere, her dad was throwing a stick to the farm's collie dog. Her sat next to her, and started humming a song. Katie thought she recognised it. She lay back on the grass and closed her eyes, the last rays of the day's sun catching her face. She couldn't remember the last time she'd felt so happy.

The peaceful sounds of her family's voices faded into the sound of singing, coming from all around her. The forest was bathed in the light of dusk, long shadows of the trees stretched off into the distance. Katie pushed herself to her feet and stumbled forward. Stumbling through a cathedral of pines, she found herself following the voices. Somewhere, in the back of her mind, she felt they were leading her. So when the huge gothic walls of the castle rose up before her, she wasn't surprised. A single light shone like a beacon from high above the wooden door.

There was no wind rustling amongst the trees, no birds chirping in the sky. Only the sound of her own footsteps accompanied her as she walked towards the castle entrance. The single light seemed to be flickering, blinking down at her like an eye, watching her every move.

Of its own accord, the ancient wooden gate creaked open as if it hadn't moved in a hundred years. She watched as rust and debris floated down past the iron bolts, settling onto large square flagstones at the base. Amongst the dust, Katie spied footprints. They looked recent. One of the prints had a familiar swoosh emblem in the centre.

'Laura?'

The footprints lead through the door into the darkness. Taking a deep breath, Katie followed.

6

The door slammed shut behind her, and an archaic gas lantern flared to life, its flames casting down into the shadows ahead. Another lantern flickered to life further on, then another, each matching Katie's steps, slowly illuminating the hallway as she walked. The walls were lined with trestle tables and old chairs. Piles of blankets were heaped up along the floor. There was a thick coat of dust over everything. Down the centre of the floor, more footprints disappeared along the way. Katie could see Laura's next to them.

'Laura?' she shouted out.

A chill wind blew down the corridor. It caught at the wet material round her legs sending a shiver down her spine. The lights began to sway above while the blankets rippled like water.

Behind her the lanterns had begun to fade out. Katie followed the footprints up a spiral stairway. As she rounded a corner, a slit in the stone walls let in a sliver of light from the outside world. She was higher up than she thought. The sun had disappeared over the horizon; its final rays glanced off the edge of the loch.

Katie continued to climb. Pictures began to appear on the staircase walls, large ornate gold frames with canvas portraits of young women. Like everything else in the castle, they showed signs of extreme age. There was something similar about each painting. They all had long dark hair, It looked like they had all been painted to the same background and they all had the same look in their eyes.

The stairs ended and Katie found herself standing before a single archway. A candle blinked in the sconce next to it.

Sudden gusts of wind from every direction made her hunker down. The candle by the door didn't even flicker. Katie looked for the source of the wind but there was nothing, no windows, no gaping holes. Nothing

The path beyond the archway was small, private. By the candlelight, she could see that the pictures lining the walls there were larger, and there were less of them. Still the same image - a young girl sitting in front of the same landscape, her eyes tight around the edges.

Suddenly, a voice said softly:

'Follow.'

Katie turned round. The picture at her side stared silently at her.

'Follow,' said another.

She spun round. The eyes of the paintings were all looking at her, terror-stricken eyes following her every move.

'What is this?' Katie tried to scream but her heart seemed to fill her throat.

'Follow,' came the sound again.

A gust of air made its way down the passage way, nudging her on. Holding onto the wall, she moved forward past the archway, and into a large hall.

From a high beamed roof, a wrought iron chandelier hung, bathing the hall in soft light. At the far end, a balcony opened out. The view beyond it was the very same background in every portrait she'd seen.

The walls of the great hall were decorated with thousands of pictures, all showing the same familiar image. She looked into their eyes, but they were no longer looking at her, but rather gazing back towards the archway where two gold frames hung. One was empty; the other held a new image.

Katie recognized the face immediately.

'Laura…'

Her eyes stared out at her, scared and alone.

'Oh Laura!' she screamed as she ran her hands over the image of her friend, tears pouring down her cheeks.

Then Katie noticed the frame next. It was empty, lying in wait for someone. Her.

Katie backed away from the wall. Her steps faltered as she spun round, ready to flee, but she turned to find herself directly facing the largest portrait in the hall. It was the image of a man, his hulking frame dressed in a great fur cloak above a kilt of red and green. From one hand hung a letter, from the other a bloody knife. His face was taut with an expression of anguish and anger. Katie felt her skin go numb. She tried pull away from his gaze but found herself moving closer.

A gust, heavy with the smell of death, blew in from the balcony, swamping through the hall and over Katie, pushing her towards that awful image.

Suddenly something else entered the hall – a thousand voices in song, echoing from the portraits. Katie began to feel new strength in her arms. She began to pull away, but rage seemed to emanate from the man's portrait, sweeping over her and sapping her strength. How could a mere picture exert this kind of force? She could feel herself falling away from her own body.

Then slowly, amongst the chorus of voices, Katie heard one she'd known all her life.

'Katie… Get up my darling… you need to be strong now. Strong for everyone.'

Her mind reeled.

'Mum...?' she gasped through the pain. 'I can't…'

'Up now Katie girl…' came her father's voice then. 'You can do it.'

Katie looked up. Figures surrounded her in the mists, and she recognized the shapes.

She pushed herself up onto her knees. The wind tore at her clothes, and waves of despair came at her from all sides. She kept her eyes on those familiar visions, drawing strength from them.

'You can't have me!' she shouted at the painting of the laird. His face seemed to her more contorted now and the grip on his knife tighter.

Katie got to her feet and against gusts stronger than any she had ever felt before, took a step backwards. The chorus of song grew exultant around her.

'Run now!' cried her parents in unison.

She turned and fled back down the passageway, back the way she had come. The lanterns flickered on an off again as she ran past.

Behind her, the laird's anguished screams echoed down the passageways. The walls around her had started to shake, and dust and debris rained down. The castle itself was coming down - the laird's final stab at her. He would take her life, one way or another.

The doorway at the end of the entrance hall shook angrily on its hinges. Wooden beams from the ceiling began to fall around her, crashing onto the stone paving with deadly force. Katie flung herself at the wooden door, its iron studs digging into her shoulder, but it wouldn't move. Balling her fists, she pounded on the ancient oak planks. Around her the building continued to fall.

Katie could feel his anger closing in on her, when suddenly another ceiling beam fell. It landed with a crack against the great door, splintering the wood around it. Fresh air wafted in and she leapt for the gap made by the beam, prying the splintered shards apart. She squeezed through the hole and out into the dark night.

Katie ran a few yards before falling onto her knees. Sucking in the cool air, she lay on her back and stared back up at the castle. Everything was silent. The structure was intact. No lights shone from the windows. It was as if nothing had happened.

She picked herself up off the ground and stumbled towards the gate.

She turned and took one last look back. The surrounding trees seemed to be swallowing the building back into the forest.

A faint voice drifted to her on the wind. It spoke softly, comforting her with a single word.

'Live.'

THE FISHERMAN'S STORM

1

The couple walked hand in hand down the steep track. The wind whipping their coats round their legs as they went. This was the trip Mark and Wendy had promised themselves for years. It was their fifth anniversary but their first honeymoon.

They had been travelling around Scotland for a few weeks, stopping at various places along the way. They'd heard from an old man about a beautiful coastal village to the east; picture post-card stuff if the man was to be believed.

The village of Leathan was at the base of a cliff, cut off from everything and the only way to get there was by an old dirt track.

They'd been walking for hours before they saw the old stone cottage. It was built only yards away from the lip of a cliff.

Everything was still but for a steady puff of smoke wafting from the house's chimney.

As they got closer they could see an old woman working in the garden, a dog lying next to her.

'Morning', said Wendy.

The old woman looked them and down.

Neither Mark nor Wendy had gotten the hang of the local hospitality yet. Often as not, a scowl could mean 'welcome' or 'move along'.

The old woman turned her head back towards the house.

'Tea',

Her thick Scots accent spat the word out like it was a hair in her mouth.

'Would you like some tea?' she spat again.

'Yes, thank you', said Wendy.

The woman got up with the help of a wooden stick and scuttled back towards the house. At the front door she stopped and rapped the walking stick three times on the front step. The dog lying by the fence got up and stretched. It walked slowly after its master.

Wendy led the way up to the house. It was a simple building and appeared to have only two areas and an outhouse round the side. The living room was dark after the bright morning light; it took their eyes some time to adjust. A fire was guttering at the back of the room, the ashes giving off a ruddy glow.

They could hear the old woman sorting the cups in the corner, a screen covered what must have been the kitchen area. Only the wagging tale of the dog was visible.

They took off their rucksacks and lay them against the wall.

'Thanks for inviting us in,' said Mark.

'Yes,' continued Wendy, 'we've been walking for hours'.

'We're trying to reach Leathan, we were told it's near here.'

The sounds from behind the screen stopped.

'Aye, it is', said the old woman.

Mark and Wendy looked at each other.

'Is it much further down the road?' asked Mark.

The old woman came out from the behind the screen holding a tray with a pot of tea, cups and what looked like cake. With a clatter she put it down on a table in the centre of the room.

'You're all but standing in the village now.' She said, 'This is the first house in Leathan.

She went about arranging the cups and saucers on the table, the cake sat in the centre next to the pot of tea. She turned to them.

'Are you going to sit down or not?'

Wendy took the seat closest to the old woman.

'Thank you again for this, I'm Wendy and this is my husband Mark. As I said, we've been walking for hours.'

For the first time, the old woman smiled.

'Aye, we're no' so close to the cities round here. You're the first visitors for many a-month.' She turned and looked out the window.

'I'm Margaret by the way, you can call me Maggie.'

Maggie poured the tea into the three delicate porcelain cups and lay them into their matching saucers.

'What's the dog's name?' asked Mark.

'Cobhair,' she said, 'she was given to my father when she was very old. Don't worry, she's a good girl and does what she's told.'

Maggie smiled again and offered them some cake. it was a thick fruit loaf, the kind that lasted for years and supposedly only gets better with age.

'What's' brought you two out this far then?' asked Maggie, 'It's an awffy long walk for a day trip.'

'It's our anniversary. Mark has always wanted to see the Highlands. I'm from Edinburgh but I moved when I was young, I haven't been back to Scotland in years. We thought we'd make a trip of it.'

'Are you from here originally?' asked Wendy.

'No,' said Maggie, 'I was born in Edinburgh but father brought us up here when we were young. I barely remember the city now.'

'Did you ever go back again, I mean to Edinburgh?' asked Wendy.

'Och no, back then that was a long way to travel and as you see for yourselves, this isn't the easiest place to get to. No no, I've been here ever since.'

They sat in an uncomfortable silence, drinking their tea.

'We should make our way down if we're hoping to get back before dark,' said Mark draining the last of his cup. 'Thanks for the tea.

Maggie nodded her head in acknowledgment.

Wendy pointed at the rucksacks by the door. Let's just go is what she meant.

Without another word, they put the bags on their backs and headed for the door.

'Maybe we'll see you two later then,' said Maggie.

At the gate they turned to see Maggie standing in the doorway.

'Watch out for the tide down there', she shouted, 'you never know what they're like at this time of year.'

With that, she closed the door.

The track became steeper as it wound its way down the cliff face. It was barely wide enough for a car but anything other than a four wheel drive would be unable to cope with the route.

They rounded a bend and were struck by the view. A natural harbour formed out of the rocks, on one end the cliffs swept round until they became a series of boulders jutting out of the sea. Like a land bridge to the ocean.

The other side ended in a sheer wall of rock, a hole eroded into the base let them see clear through to the other side. Nestled between these was the village of Leathan.

Twenty or thirty small white house's neatly joined to one another.

From where they stood they could see some men on a small wooden pier working. Boats had been tied all along and were gently bobbing up and down in the current.

A small beach ran along the water's edge where yellow sand met the water right up to the end of the bay.

Wendy turned round and planted a kiss on Mark's cheek.

'Thank you for this, for convincing me to come… I feel better already'

Taking each other's hands, they continued down the old dirt track.

Mark looked out at the ocean. A dark cloud was heading their way.

'Honey,' he said, 'I'm sorry to say but we may not be able to spend much time here;

that cloud looks like it's heading straight for here and It could take us a while to get back to the main road.'

'We'll spend fifteen minutes and then I'll race you back up to the main road. Deal?'

'Deal', laughed Mark.

The track wound down to the base of the cliff, over a small metal bridge. A trickle of water ran down the wall of rock to their left.

While Wendy stopped to take some pictures, Mark stood looking at the approaching clouds. It was going to be a wet walk back to the road.

The cliff soared above them, disappearing into the distance where it dropped back into the sea. The village appeared to back right onto the base of, their chimneys part of the rock face. Each had a small garden to the front.

'Can I help?'

The strong smell of stale sweat and old fish wafted over them. A man stood directly behind. He was small and wore a dirty baseball cap.

'Sorry, we've just arrived,' said Wendy.

The man looked up at her, his eyes lingering on her breasts.

'No worries darlin', said the man, 'we're no used to getting folks down here, always a bit o' interest ken? See for y'rselves.'

He nodded his head in the direction of the houses. Already several doors had opened, and Mark could feel the eyes of the village looking on suspiciously.

'Told you', said the man

Mark turned back to him.

He gave Mark a look of contempt.

'No worries pal,' he said, 'you'll no find any problems here. you'll probably be the talk o' the place for months to come.

He turned back to Wendy.

'If y' need anything, just look for Mikey.

He shuffled off towards the pier, turning back to leer at Wendy every few steps.

'Mikey huh?' said Mark.

'Shh, somebody else is coming.'

A woman was striding down the main street towards them. She clearly held herself aloof. She had all the bearings of a head mistress.

Wendy grabbed Mark's hand and walked up to the woman.

'Afternoon,' said Wendy.

'Afternoon' said the woman back. 'Welcome to Leathan. My name is Mrs

Elizabeth Grath. I'm the council elder for the village.

She spoke as if addressing dignitaries, curt and formal.

'Hi there, I'm Mark Atholl and this is my wife…'

'…Wendy,' Said Mrs Grath.

They looked at each other surprised.

A shadow of a smile crept onto the woman's face.

'I just had a telephone call from Margaret. She said to expect you.'

Mrs Grath stopped and looked at the clouds over the sea.

'Let me give you a tour of the village before the rain sets in.'

Mark stopped and looked around, the sky turning grey overhead.

'Thanks for the offer Mrs Grath but I'm afraid we were trying to get back to the main road before the rain hit.'

Mark turned to Wendy.

'Right honey?'

Wendy looked at the rain clouds, disappointment clear in her eye.

'I think we'll give the road back a try. I hope we can come back another time though. It really is so beautiful.'

'Thank you,' she said, 'but you'll find it more difficult than you think getting back to the road.'

For a second Wendy thought she saw a smile cross the woman's lips. Something about it made her uncomfortable.

'If you find yourselves back in Leathan,' continued Mrs Grath, 'I'm in the second house from the end. You'll be more than welcome.'

With that, she started back down the road towards the houses.

They pulled up their hoods and started back towards the dirt track.

The heavens opened as they made their way back up. Rain poured down in sheets, drenching them immediately.

Mark took Wendy's hand and pulled her along behind him.

They rounded the bend onto the old metal bridge and stopped, Water poured a hundred feet above down over the path.

Mark could feel the metal under his feet shake with the force of the water. There was no way to cross. They were trapped.

2

They sat in the lounge of Mrs Grath's house. The weather howled outside. Waves crashed over the harbour showering the houses with sea spray.

Mrs Grath was on the phone in another room; she had seemed genuinely sorry for them when they appeared on her door step. She'd said it was a regular occurrence and would die down in no time. That was three hours ago.

Wendy stood looking out the window, a blanket draped over her shoulders.

Mrs Grath had given them both a warm welcome when they showed up. Soft warm towels to dry off and all the tea you could want.

Mark sat next to an electric fire, a hot mug clasped between his hands.

'Is it looking any better out there?' he asked.

'No,' Said Wendy, not turning from the window. 'it looks like it's getting worse.'

Even if the rain stopped now, it would be dark by the time they found the main road again and it would be pure luck if there were any buses running.

Then Mrs Grath walked back in.

'I'm afraid they've just announced a storm alert.' She said.

Mark slammed his cup down on the table.

'Should they not have announced that hours ago?' his voice rising.

Mrs Grath looked at him calmly. She picked up the cup next to Marks and handed it to Wendy.

'Drink this dear, no sense you picking up a cold too.'

Mrs Grath turned and sat down next to Mark.

'Mr Atholl', she said facing Mark, 'what you're seeing out there isn't really a storm for us, just a regular squall. If you look out, you'll see the fishermen still hard at work sorting the day's catch.'

She looked over to the window.

'A storm here is a different thing entirely. Right now, all the houses in Leathan are preparing for a long night and I think you and your wife should too.'

Mark's shoulders slump.

'I'm sorry, I didn't mean to shout.' He said, 'but is there nobody here with a car? We would be happy to pay the owner the petrol money to get us to Aberdeen or even the nearest bus station.'

Mrs Grath picked up a cup of tea for herself and leaned back in the chair.

'You've been down the track yourself Mr Atholl,' she explained, 'when dry it's difficult, during a storm it's impassable.'

She sipped her tea.

'No car has been up or down there in years. Now we use the boats to bring in supplies. Anybody needing to get to the city must do that way.'

Mark looked up suddenly but Mrs Grath held up her hands before he could speak.

'No Mr Atholl, our fishermen will not take you either. You would be asking them to risk their lives, and for what?'

Mrs Grath looked Mark straight in the eyes.

'…So you and your wife can sleep in a warm bed away from the big bad storm…'

Mark looked over to his wife, she hadn't moved from the window. He gestured for Mrs Grath to lean closer.

'Mrs Grath, it's not as simple as that. I fully appreciate what you're telling me but please understand. My wife hasn't been well. I just want her to be ok.

Mrs Grath leaned back, her hands crossed on her lap.

'You shouldn't have brought your wife here Mr Atholl.' She whispered. 'Leathan is no place for the ill; we're isolated here.

Mrs Grath turned to Wendy.

'Mrs Atholl, come and sit. I really wouldn't want you catching a cold.'

Wendy turned and took a seat on the other side of the fire.

Mrs Grath looked at both of them, the head mistress look returning.

'Right, with the storm on the way, you'll have to stay in the village tonight. '

'I have already made arrangements for you to stay with the Cairn's; they live a few doors down.'

Mrs Grath began to pour more tea when they heard the sound of a dog barking outside the front door, followed by a scratching on the wood.

The woman sighed and stood up.

'She's going to kill herself one of these days,' she said speaking to no one in particular.

She walked over and opened the door. In burst a soaking wet dog followed quickly by Maggie. Cobhair immediately jumped up onto Mark, tail wagging furiously. Three sharp raps of Maggie's walking stick on the stone floor brought the dog back to her heel.

Grath stood facing her.

'Maggie, I told you I would meet you and we would walk down together. You could have been taken over by the falls.'

The old woman waved Grath aside.

'Nonsense Lizzy,' she said. 'I've been crossing those falls since you were a girl and nothing has happened that I've no recovered from.'

She then turned and pointed her stick at Mark and Wendy.

'I see you two have got yourselves stuck.'

Maggie looked as if she had more to say but was cut short by Grath pulling her into the kitchen. Cobhair ran through after them.

Mark moved his chair closer to his wife; she was staring into the bars of the electric fire, a soft hum emanating from the machine.

'I know what you're thinking,' she said. 'But I'm fine, I promise.'

'Are you sure?' he asked. 'I don't know what it is but I don't think we're being told everything.

'I know,' said Wendy, 'let's not piss them off though. They're helping us for the moment.'

Wendy took Mark's hand and squeezed it reassuringly.

'I need to use the little girl's room,' she said suddenly.

Wendy walked over and knocked on the door Mrs Grath and Maggie had gone through.

'Come on in dears,' came a voice.

Wendy opened the door. The two women were standing close together, and there was a strange tension in the room.

'Could I use your bathroom Mrs Grath?' asked Wendy.

'Of course dear,' she replied. 'It's the room to the rear of the hallway, last on the right.

Wendy thanked her and left. She blew a kiss to Mark as she went through the door. It was total darkness inside the hallway.

'I can't find the light switch,' said Wendy.

Mark looked up from his seat by the fire.

'It's on this side,' he said.

Wendy flicked the switch; a weak bulb flickered to life above her. She turned to Mark.

'Better than nothing I suppose.'

<u>3</u>

Wendy closed the door and made her way to the bathroom. The hallway was dark and narrow, old pictures hung on the walls.

Inside, she stood by the sink and ran cold water over her face. She turned round when she heard footsteps outside her door.

'I'm in here,' she cried out.

'You're it…'

Wendy looked up.

It was just a whisper but she was sure it was a child's voice.

'Hello?'

She turned off the taps and listened. The room grew silent. She walked over to the door and pressed her ear to the wood.

She could hear light footsteps on the other side. They were running away.

Wendy opened the door. The light had gone out and the hallway was in darkness.

'Mark?' she shouted. 'Switch the light back on'.

There was no answer.

She started walking back up the hall. Behind her the floor boards creaked. She spun round. A shaft of light glowed from beneath a door at the back of the hallway. The light flickered as something ran across the floor inside.

And then she heard something laugh - a little girl.

Wendy moved back towards the door when she heard a man's voice.

'NO!' it shouted.

The light flickered out leaving Wendy alone in the dark. Suddenly the bulb above her switched on.

Mark stood in the open door behind her.

'You alright?' he asked. 'You've been gone ages'.

'I think there are other people here, children,' she whispered. 'I think I heard them just then.'

Mark nodded.

'Maybe she runs the village school from here,' he joked. 'Where else are they going to go every day, unless they get in a boat every morning?'

'I suppose so…'

They were sitting down as Mrs Grath and Maggie walked back into the room.

'Ok you two,' said Grath. 'I think we should get you over to the Cairns before the storm gets any worse.'

Mark fetched their back packs from the corner of the room.

Wendy stood up and walked over to a picture on the wall.

Written on a brass plaque along the bottom was 'Leathan Village – June 1946'; the photo showed a group of men and women standing in front of the houses; behind them children were playing in the street.

'This is a lovely picture Mrs Grath,' said Wendy.

Mrs Grath stood by her shoulder.

'It was a beautiful day,' she said. 'Many of the village men were just back from the war and they had landed their first catch that morning. We were all so happy.'

Mrs Grath pointed to a small girl sitting in a doorway; a doll lay in her lap. She was smiling at the camera.

'That was me,' said Mrs Grath. We were all given the morning off school so we could help with the welcome party. It really was such a beautiful day.'

There was something in the old woman's voice. Something like remorse, or a terrible sadness. The old woman was staring at the photo; tears in her eyes.

Wendy wanted to ask what had happened but a loud bark from Cobhair made them both jump. Grath gave the dog a sharp look.

'Leave it be,' said Maggie from across the room. 'There'll be time for that later. Let's get these two down the road.'

She turned to the couple.

'Both of you!' she said facing the couple, 'Put your water proofs on, you'll need them out there.'

Mrs Grath showed them to the door, all traces of sadness gone from her face.

'Maggie will show you down to the Cairns herself' she said.

'We'll all eat together. When a storm is expected the whole village has dinner in the church. It's our way.'

She looked at Wendy.

'Both of you should try and get some rest while you're there. The Cairns won't mind. I'll send someone to pick you up for dinner in a few hours.'

She opened the door for them all to leave.

Maggie popped open an umbrella and walked out, three raps from her cane echoing from behind. Cobhair moved quickly out the door.

They followed her down the path, thanking Mrs Grath one more time for her help.

The clouds rolled above them and lightening flashed across the sky.

Wendy stayed close to Mark. The sea broke against the rocky harbour next to them. The spray off the waves left a salty tang on their lips.

Maggie silently marched ahead of them, her umbrella held high. She paid little to no heed of the deluge she was walking through. Cobhair walked between the group, occasionally stopping to look back before returning to Maggie's side.

Each house they passed had a small front garden, decorated to the owners personal preference, but all very similar. Materials for fishing could be seen everywhere. Nets hung from most of the fences, if it wasn't a net, it was a creel or fishing rod; ready to be used at a moment's notice. Wendy pointed this out to Mark.

'What do you think?' she had to shout over the wind. 'Somewhere to live?'

He looked at her, rain dripping off his nose.

'I think it would smell,' he shouted back.

Wendy rolled her eyes and took his hand.

On the far side of the village the rising moon shone through the centre of the eroded cliff. A flash of lightening lit up the bay. Standing in the centre of the stone circle was a child, a little girl. She stood perilously close to the edge. The tide threatened to drag her to the depths.

Wendy shouted to Maggie but the wind swallowed her cry. She looked back at the child. She was staring at them now, a hollow look in her young eyes.

Suddenly a wave crashed over them. Wendy wiped the spray from her eyes.

The child was gone.

<u>4</u>

They stopped outside of the house where a fishing rod lay unused on a bench.

Maggie opened the gate and rapped the front door with her cane.

Nobody answered. She rapped again, harder.

'Come on Cairns, wake up!' Maggie shouted through the letter box.

After a few moments, the door began to open. She pushed it the rest of the way with her foot. An old smiling face told them to come in and make themselves at home.

The house was almost a replica of Mrs Grath's house up the road, a living room with a kitchen off to the side. A door in the back led to the rest of the house.

They walked into the main lounge room; it had more furniture than Mrs Grath's giving it a warmer atmosphere.

Mr Cairns looked impossibly old. He walked with a cane and wore a patched cardigan. His thinning hair was swept into a comb-over.

He took their jackets from them as soon as they got in.

Maggie was speaking to someone in the other room. Cobhair was in the corner of the room chewing a pair of slippers.

After a few minutes, she came back out followed by a frail old woman.

They both shuffled up to Wendy.

'How you feeling lass?'

Wendy looked up quickly.

'…Oh fine… just…' she tried to say.

'…We know you're not too well lass, don't worry. Nothing wrong with that.'

Wendy turned red, trying to smile.

'Just to give you a wee word to the wise.'

Maggie moved a little closer to Wendy.

'This isn't an ideal place to fall ill, ok? We're fair isolated round here and this storm only makes it worse.'

'Don't worry, I understand.'

'I doubt that very much.' Maggie interrupted. 'Listen, you may see or hear some strange things tonight, at the dinner. Just let it be and you'll be alright. Just us crazy old buggers keeping ourselves amused. It just looks a little strange to an outsider. Understand?'

Wendy nodded her head.

'Maggie,' she said, 'I thought I saw a little girl playing at the end of the bay, at the cliff edge.'

The old woman's eyes sharpened momentarily.

'Yes,' continued Wendy. 'I was worried. I heard the other children at Mrs Grath's house. I thought maybe she'd gone outside.'

Maggie stepped back slightly, her knuckles turning white round her cane.

'Don't you worry about that lass,' she said, 'nothing to worry about. Just you remember what I said.'

She turned, her hand already stretching for the door knob.

'I'll see you all in a few hours. I'll send Mikey to pick you all up.'

She opened the door and walked off into the gale, Cobhair running along after her.

Wendy closed the door behind her. The Cairns had barely noticed she'd left. They were busy arranging the chairs round the fire.

Wendy took a mug of tea and sat down next to the window. Lightening flickered outside. She could see Maggie walking back in the direction they'd come from.

The old woman stopped in the middle of the street, the rain and wind pounding at her. She stared out at the stone outcrop for what seemed an age before making her way back up the road.

5

An hour had passed and they were all sitting in the front room by the fire. Mark was sitting next to his Wendy. She'd fallen asleep in the chair not long after Maggie left. He finished his third cup of tea and stretched. The heat in the small room was stifling and he was trying not to doze off himself. The Cairns were in the kitchen talking amongst themselves.

Mark stood and walked round the room; pictures lined every wall. They were similar to the ones hanging on Mrs Grath's wall.

Many of them had children running around in the background, some with adults some without. But he couldn't remember seeing anything remotely toy-like around the village when they'd arrived.

Mrs Cairns walked back into the room, a fresh tray of tea in her hands. She stopped and looked down at the sleeping Wendy.

'Poor dear' she said. 'You must both be exhausted from all this.'

She put the tray on the table and disappeared through a door behind her. A moment later she came back out with a blanket. She draped it gently over Wendy, He smiled a thanks the old woman.

She turned to him.

'We're just making us a wee sandwich, after you can go through and take five minutes to yourselves. We'll knock when Mikey comes.'

'That would be great' said Mark, 'Thank you again for doing this. I really hope we're not putting you both out too much.'

'No no dear,' she said shuffling off towards the kitchen. 'It's been a long time

213

since we had some young people round here to talk with.'

She laughed as she opened the kitchen door.

'Gives us old duds something to gossip about for the next 6 months'

Mark heard the two of them laugh in the kitchen.

Mrs Cairns' comment left him thinking again. 'Long time since we had young people round here' she'd said.

The couple came back into the room carrying plates of sandwiches between them.

Outside, while the weather continued to rage, they spoke quietly about past storms and the damage they could do. Mr Cairns laughed as he spoke about the year he found the top of his own boat in the front garden. The hull was still moored out in the bay.

'What if somebody is injured during a storm?' asked Mark. 'What happens if one of the children gets hurt?'

This question was met with silence.

'There have been incidents here over the years' said the old man. 'We've lost many people to the weather here. It's part of a fisherman's life though, the risk.'

Mr Cairns stopped, his eyes swept over the pictures on the walls.

'Friends and family have always played an important part in Leathan; often as not they're one in the same thing. When you lose one, the other's gone too.'

Mark sat waiting for him to continue.

The howling wind shook the windows of the small house making him feel claustrophobic.

Mr Cairns was looking at a particular picture on the wall. It was the same one hanging in Mrs Grath's house.

'It was the year after the war and all our fathers had come back from fighting. When they came back we were so happy. The whole village was happy; all the men who'd left those years before had all come back in one piece. Many others were less fortunate.'

'The first day they came back from the fishing with a big catch', Mr Cairn had a smile on his face as he spoke. 'We had a party. Every house in Leathan was decorated to the nines. All the children were playing in the street while the adults ate from a long table outside; I got to sit next to my dad while he drank whiskey and told us stories from when he was away. In the evening, somebody turned the radio on and we all got to dance. I sat with the other children, we were drinking hot toddies to ward off the chill but our parents all kept dancing. I remember the look on their faces; everybody was so happy. It was one of the best days of my life.'

His smile faded.

'I don't know what time it was when the wind picked up but it was agreed the party was over. Everybody was to lend a hand clearing up, even the children. The weather changed so quickly that night; the wind turned in to a gale while the rain poured down on us. Lightening forked across the ocean in front us while the thunder crashed overhead. I'd never seen anything like it, not to this day.

'The men of the village all left to secure the boats while the women and children picked up the last of the tables and chairs; I was inside with my mother when it happened. We lay our things down in this very room when we heard the rumbling, I asked my mother what it was but she didn't know. It got so loud that the room started

217

to shake. She ran for the front door, but it slammed closed before she could get to it. The whole house shook so violently, we were knocked to the floor by the force of it. The windows smashed in and water came poured in. We held onto each other for God knows how long; maybe one minute, maybe an hour.

'Then, everything went silent.

'We crept out the front door, it was so calm. There were no lights left in the village but we could see by the moon that nothing remained.

'My mother clung to the wall as she made her way down the street, I followed close behind. Another woman was making her way out of a house at the far end, she started calling out names. Nobody answered.

'Fishing nets were caught in the trees, even over the houses. I couldn't stop staring at them. Something was caught up in amongst one of them. It hung there limp, swinging in the breeze.

'Soon after, lights across the village blinked into life. Someone had managed to kick some life into the old backup generator. My mother told me to stay where I was by the wall. I remember looking up back up at the net, at the thing hanging there.

'Two dead eyes staring down at me. My father's. I don't remember much after that. The storm took everything from us that night.'

Mr Cairns looked over at his wife.

'Only five of us bairns survived the storm, the men and the other wee ones were never found. My father was the only villager to be buried, the rest were taken by the storm.'

<u>6</u>

'I'm so sorry' said Wendy.

Mark turned, he hadn't seen her wake up.

Mr Cairns stretched his legs out in front of him and took hold of his wife's hand. She was sound asleep . He smiled kindly at Mark and Wendy.

'Maybe now you'll forgive us Leathan folk any quirks we have. We've had to learn to live a certain way here and it's not always obvious why we do these things.'

He turned to his wife and gently shook her.

'Come my love, time we napped before the meal.'

He helped his wife to her feet.

'I'm sure you two could do with a quick five minutes, I'll take you to the spare room.

They were shown to a room on the left, near the end of the hall. Inside they were surprised to find a double bed with a nightstand ready and waiting for them, their bags lay at the foot of the bed while the wet jackets hung in an airing closet on the other side.

Mark sat on the edge of the bed, preparing to take his shoes off.

'I can't get over that story. Why do they all stay here after something like that? It's crazy.'

'He said it himself' said Wendy. They have their quirks. It must have brought everyone together in a way;

'Maybe your right,' he said. 'still...'

Mark smiled at Wendy and patted the duvet.

Within minutes, they were both sound asleep.

Mark woke up with a start. He'd dreamed about the storm, he'd been surrounded by children but there was something wrong with them. Their eyes…

He rubbed his hands over his face and slid quietly out of the bed, he looked back to his wife, she was sleeping soundly. He kissed her on the forehead before going in search of a toilet.

As the bedroom door closed behind him, Mark noticed a light coming from beneath a door at the rear of the hall. Somebody was walking pacing in front of the door, he could see the shadow against the glow.

He crept closer but heard nothing. He took a few steps back when suddenly he heard the sound of footsteps. Not wanting to appear rude, he went and knocked quietly on the door.

'Mr Cairns?... Mrs Cairns? It's Mark…'

There was no reply and the footsteps had stopped again. Mark turned the handle on the door, opening it a crack.

'Hello?'…' Whispered Mark.

Mark opened the door a little more, it was empty. The room was nearly the same size as the living room and bedrooms together. Painted white walls gleamed in comparison to the rest of the house. More surprising was the back of the room, Mark thought it was painted a different colour before taking a closer look. He walked over and ran his hand down, it was rough stone. Dry lichen still clung to some areas.

It was the base of the cliff. He looked up in astonishment, it ran all the way down and met with the wooden floor boards of the house. It was perfectly sealed against the outside world. Mark took a step back. a large wooden door stood in the middle of the cliff face, it was rounded at the top and had metal bands running horizontally along its width. Mark's mind was reeling.

'What is this place?' he thought. 'A pantry? Cellar?'

He turned to inspect the rest of the room when a sound came from behind the door in the cliff. Footsteps.

He leaned up against the wood and listened, the steps seemed to be moving away.

Mark succumbed to his curiosity. He turned the iron handle of the door and opened it.

A blast of cold air hit him in the face. A tunnel had been cut into the rock itself, it stretched back into the cliff into darkness. A string of light bulbs hung loosely from the ceiling, they swung as the wind from inside gusted. Mark flicked a switch next to the door but nothing happened. The floor of the cliff was covered in stone chips.

Mark heard something else. It sounded like more footsteps, this time walking on gravel. He stepped inside, craning his head so he could hear better. He heard it again. This time it was closer. Mark thought about calling out but something stopped him. He was afraid.

Another footstep, crunching heavily back towards the tunnel entrance. They were getting quicker, as if whatever they belonged to had picked up a scent. Another gust of wind burst down the tunnel over him. Mark backed away from the darkness.

The sounds of footsteps were nearly running now. He was sure they were nearly on him when he slammed the wooden door closed. The sound echoed in the empty room. Mark could feel his heart pumping in his chest. He stared at the door in the cliff, half expecting it to open itself.

Mark turned and left the room, his hands shaking

As he opened the bedroom door he looked back. Shadowy footsteps paced back and forth In front of the door again.

7

Back in the bedroom, Mark sat down on a chair facing the double bed, Wendy was still sleeping. She had mentioned something about children back at Mrs Graths, he was shaking again. He didn't like this place, something didn't feel right.

He lay back down on the bed and held Wendy in his arms.

They awoke to the sound of knocking on their door. Mark wasn't sure how long they'd been sleeping for but he felt a lot better.

'Hullo!' came the voice of Mr Cairns, 'It is almost time to go. We'll be waiting in the front room for you'.

'Ok thank you,' said Mark. 'We'll be right through.'

He gently shook his wife and she stretched her arms above her head.

'Alright,' she said, 'let's get this over with.'

Mark noticed that as she pulled her shoes back on, she seemed distracted.

'Everything alright?'

'Yes, fine,' she replied. 'Just an upset stomach is all.'

They made their way out of the room, past the hallway light flickering on and off. Mark looked back at the at the rear door of the hallway. It was silent.

He took Wendy's hand and they made their way out to the living room.

Two cups of tea were lying there ready for them and Mr and Mrs Cairns were sitting quietly by the fire. The storm raged on outside.

Before long, the door shook with three heavy knocks. Mr Cairns took his cane and walked over. He'd barely opened it when

Mikey barged in, wearing a heavy raincoat with the hood up over his baseball cap. He strode over to the table and grabbed one of the cups of tea without asking.

'It's pissin' doon out there,' he said taking a loud slurp from the mug. 'Are yous' nearly ready?'

Mikey leered at Wendy.

'How's the visitors getting on, you enjoying y'r wee stay?'

He laughed as he said it, an unpleasant laugh like someone hacking on a fishbone.

'The Cairns have been very kind to us, thanks,' said Wendy stiffly. 'Haven't they Mark?.'

Mark stepped in front of Mikey, blocking the view of his wife.

'They've been great,' he said. 'Maybe we should head on over to the meal now. Don't want to keep everybody waiting.'

229

Wendy moved over to Mrs Cairns who had dozed off again. She bent down and took the old woman's elbow, her eyes fluttered open.

Mikey had moved back over to the door, a look of contempt on his face; he snorted back another laugh as he watched the old couple.

'Come on then,' he said, 'the storm'll be over by the time you two get on with it.'

Mark started to say something and then he felt a hand on his shoulder.

'Leave it be,' said Mr Cairns gently.

Mikey laughed his fishbone laugh again. He turned and wretched open the door, and a cold wind suddenly raced through the house sending bits of paper everywhere. He shoved his hands in his pockets and walked out into the gale, leaving the others to wrestle the door closed.

They walked with their hands on the fence, bracing every step against the storm. The only light came from some sparsely placed lanterns hanging from a wire stretched the length of the entire village.

Mark brought up the rear of their party. Mr Cairns was up front with Wendy helping Mrs Cairns. Mikey was already far down the street, a stream of cigarette smoke wafting from inside the raincoat.

The waves crashed off to their left. The sound felt like somebody was hitting a drum next to their ears. Every few minutes they would be swamped up to the ankles as the water broke past the harbour wall. The force was almost enough to take all four of them into the sea.

Slowly they made it past the last house in the village. Mark could see the track back up to the top of the cliff. Dark, muddy water ran down it like a river. It spilt out over the cobblestone path and out into the vast rolling sea.

They were led further down the harbour, headed towards something resembling a church. They started over a bridge, its rails slick with the rain. Run off from the waterfall overhead spilt over them, pulling at their legs.

The roar from the falls was deafening. It was like a nightmare. He watched as Wendy struggled to get Mrs Cairns over the bridge, the old woman kept slipping on the rain soaked planks. Mr Cairns held his cane out for her to hold, his voice pleading with her to grab on but she couldn't hear. The rain pounded on the metal bridge drowning out all other sounds. He watched in horror as a sudden gust of wind took Wendy's legs out from beneath her. Like a chain Mr and Mrs Cairns went down too. The three were on the verge of being washed into the sea below.

Suddenly a torch was shining in their faces, and silhouettes stood all around them, hands trying to help Mark to balance.

'Not me, them. Get them!' he shouted.

They were hustled off the bridge and into the church. Mark had never been so happy to be back inside.

<u>8</u>

They were sat on a wooden bench by the wall, their rescuers standing around them.

Mikey was by the door, where another villager in a raincoat stood talking to him, their hoods both pulled up.

Mark turned to Wendy.

'Are you alright?

'Just a little drenched,' she smiled. 'I think that storm was a first for me, how about you?'

The villager talking to Mikey walked over and uncovered her head. It was Mrs Grath and she wasn't looking happy.

'I have to apologise for Mikey,' she said, 'He should've walked with you the whole way. We always walk with the group.'

Mark took in his surroundings. They sat in the vestry, crates and boxes marked with food brands towered over them and extended all over. He guessed they kept most of their winter food stores here. A path had been left between the crates so they could get through to the main church hall.

Something cold touched his hand, Cobhair was sitting next to him; his tail wagging slowly.

'Hello again you two,' said a familiar voice. It was Maggie.

'I heard you were left to fend for yourselves out there.'

She turned pointed her cane accusingly at the scowling man by the door.

'They would have been better with an old crone like me leading them here! Go out and make sure the generators have enough fuel. maybe a little more rain'll make you think clearer'.

Mikey did as he was told, his face like thunder.

'NO!' shouted Mrs Grath, 'We don't send our people back out into the storm, it's too dangerous'.

Maggie turned to Mrs Grath, anger flashing in her eyes.

'He's never been one of *our people*, has he?'

Mrs Grath stepped forward.

'Mikey, go to the hall and help with the food and be quick about it.'

She kept her eyes fixed on Maggie as she said it.

The baseball cap slinked off between the crates.

Maggie turned and went off without saying another word. The other villagers followed her through.

'I'm sorry about that' said Mrs Grath. 'We're like a family here and sometimes, we have our disagreements. Most of mine are with Maggie.

Mrs Grath smiled.

'She's like the older sister I never had.'

The couple nodded in understanding.

'I'm sorry we're causing so many problems' said Wendy standing up. 'I should have been looking after Mrs Cairns better…'

'You couldn't have done any more than the rest of us out there,' said Mrs Grath. 'Mikey should have warned you though. He's not the most reliable and I'd like nothing more than to…' She shrugged. 'Well… unfortunately he's needed.'

'Why's that?' asked Mark.

'It's simple really. He's the only one able to manage boats now. The rest of us are all too old. He came in from one of the other villages years ago, he didn't have a great reputation but he arrived when we were in dire straits.'

Mrs Grath led them through the piles of crates and into the main chapel. It was huge; hundreds of candles in sconces lit the massive room. Where usually you'd find pews, trestle tables lined the hall. A giant, ornate fire place had been built into the wall.

Mark tried to hide his surprised look. The hall was similar in design to the back room at the Cairns. Two doors were built directly into the wall either side of the fire place. The cliff face again seemed to be the main structure.

The other villagers already sat at the tables. They all appeared to be in their sixties at least.

There wasn't a child in sight.

Mrs Grath ushered them to the middle table. They could feel the eyes of the villagers on them as they took their seats.

Slowly they began to feel the heat come back into their bodies, they were each given a glass of hot wine and told to relax and enjoy themselves.

After a few minutes Mrs Grath stood up. The room went silent.

'I would like to welcome our guests this evening' she said to the whole room. 'They came down earlier this afternoon to have a look at the village and unfortunately got caught out by the local weather.'

A chuckle rippled out from the rest of the villagers.

'So' she continued, 'I would like you all to welcome them to our gathering for the storm outside.'

Mrs Grath raised her glass at the couple, the rest of the room followed.

'And now we must remember why we sit here.'

She took her wine glass in both hands and lowered her head as if in prayer.

'Never to forget the things that have been lost to us or those, no matter how cherished or beloved. We shall always be here for our lost ones, tending to your sorrows and minding to your young. One day we will all be together again.'

A gust of wind raced through the chapel, sending the candles flickering.

Mark kept his head down while Mrs Grath spoke. It wasn't any of the usual prayers he'd heard.

He felt uneasy in the silence that followed, it was as if the villagers were awaiting an answer to something.

After a few moments the villagers began to talk amongst themselves again and food started to arrive.

The dinner was large. Platters were brought to each table for starters, mains and desserts.

By the time the last plate had been cleared, they were stuffed and feeling drowsy.

Mrs Grath sat down next to Wendy.

'How are you getting on?' she asked. 'If you can't eat any more, just say.'

Wendy laughed.

Mrs Grath looked back at Mark. He was playing with Cobhair under the table and feeding him leftovers.

He saw Mrs Grath's face turn serious as she took Wendy's hand.

'And how are you feeling? She said. 'I hear you managed to get some sleep earlier.'

'Yes I'm fine, I think.' Said Wendy 'still a little tired but that could be to do with the food.'

Mrs Grath sat looking into Wendy's eyes. Mark could see it made her uncomfortable, like she was waiting for her to say something.

'Mr Cairn's told us about the storm all those years ago, the one that almost destroyed the village.'

Mrs Grath let go of her hand suddenly and looked around the hall.

'Yes, that was our lowest moment; my own father was taken by the storm. It left many of the villagers without anybody.'

She gazed off into the fire at the back of the hall.

'You're right when you say it nearly destroyed the village; many of them wanted to leave Leathan. It was my mother who convinced everybody to stay... 'This is our home, our history'... she would say. She'd lost as much as anybody yet she stayed. Others still packed up and left. I think my mother felt betrayed.'

She spat out the last word.

'…My mother told me what had to be done for the village to survive… they were hard measures but it ensured we would always have our homes and our village. Before my mother died, she told me people wouldn't like it but that they had to obey or who knows what would happen…'

Mrs Grath's words didn't seem aimed at them. The words were full of anger and sorrow. There was determination there too, realised Mark. Whatever had to be done, she would do it.

'Have some wine Mrs Grath,' said Wendy trying to bring the woman back.

Wendy touched the rim of her own glass to hers.

'To you and Leathan, without it, I don't know what Mark and I would have done.'

Mrs Grath smiled at the toast and bowed her head slightly. She smiled at the two of them, something about the gesture didn't seem right. As if she knew something they didn't.

'You'll have to excuse me,' she said rising to her feet 'there are a few things I need to see to.'

She stood up and went through on of the doors at the back of the hall.

9

They sat staring at the fire for a few moments, lost in the events unfolding around them.

They turned when they heard a discreet cough from behind.

Maggie sat across from them staring.

She picked up a glass of wine and swirled the dark liquid around the edges.

'Were you talking to Grath about the storm?' She said the name as if it were something sour in her mouth. 'Careful of that topic round here. That storm ruined many lives here.

'Mr Cairns told us about it earlier this afternoon' said Mark. 'Is it really so fresh in everybody's minds?'

'Look around you. Everybody here lost something or someone to that storm.'

She looked up into the vaulted ceiling.

'I was a teenager when it happened. I saw the wave through the window; the spray hit the cliff so hard I felt the ground beneath my feet shake. My father had been down in the village helping to clean up, he sent me back up the cliff with firewood. That was the last time I saw him.'

Maggie took a sip of her wine.

'I spent that night on the floor, scared that something would come back. I never knew what happened until the next morning.

'Strange. It was a beautiful day, the waves lapped at the shore and there wasn't a cloud in the sky. The sun shone off the houses making them glow as if they'd only been built last week. I remember it all seemed so serene, so quiet and peaceful.

'Then I heard the crying. Some wept openly in the streets, others stood up to their waists in the sea, calling out names but getting no answer.

Someone had taken paradise and up-ended it into hell.'

Maggie leaned back and took a bottle of wine from the table. It was half empty by the time she was done with it.

'Only Grath's mother did anything' she continued, 'made everybody get back up and work before the weather could turn again. No one was excused. Even her daughter was made to work. In the end, I think that's what killed her. She lost as much as anybody that night but she was the one who put her all into getting us back. She even presided over the burials…'

Mark looked up.

'… I thought they were all taken by the sea, except Mr Cairns' father?'

Maggie downed another drink.

'That's what we told some of the younger ones,' she said. 'Mr Cairns' father was the first to be found. The others started washing up over the next few days, men and children.

'Grath's mother told us to collect the bodies and hide them where they wouldn't be found, for the sake of the village…'

'How could you do it?' said Mark, 'how could you make yourself…?'

'You never knew the former Mrs Grath,' snapped Maggie. 'You did what you were told or you would regret it later. We did what we were told and that was it.'

Mark stared into his own empty glass. He thought back to the room in the Cairn's house.

'What about the children? He asked.

Maggie slammed her glass down on the table, shattering the base.

248

'What about them?' barked Maggie.

She turned to Wendy suddenly.

'Leathan is a dead place, has been for years. Take your pictures while you can kids cause it won't be around much longer. Too much has happened.'

Maggie stood up and left.

Mark turned to his wife

'Do you believe her?'

'I don't know,' said Wendy quietly.

Mark told her about the room at the back of the Cairns house.

When he finished, she grabbed his hand and squeezed hard.

'Mrs Grath reckons we'll be able to get out by tomorrow morning. All we need to do is hold out till then, ok.'

Mark nodded. He didn't want her to know how terrified he was.

10

They were back in the vestry of the church. The villagers of Leathan stood around them, ready for the all clear to leave the building.

Mark felt like he was back in the school playground, standing in columns holding hands waiting on the teacher telling them to go back into the classroom. Mrs Grath stood by the door and looked down the line, checking to see everybody was there.

Maggie stood outside the group, swaying slightly. Cobhair walked unnoticed around the room.

Mrs Grath walked over to them.

'The storm is too bad for everybody to be walking separately so we'll be going in a group, I'll take the first lot, Mikey will lead the second. He'll do what he's told this time.'

Mikey heaved the massive door open. The weather burst into the room, like a wild animal it raced through the room dragging at the people inside.

Mrs Grath signalled for everybody to get moving, she and Maggie stood arm in arm as the first group shuffled out the door, they disappeared into a swirl of rain and wind; the two old women trailed along after them.

'Your turn,' shouted Mikey through the gale.

The column moved together towards the door. Mark gripped his wife's hand tightly. They walked slowly towards the oncoming darkness.

Outside, the gale swallowed everything that came into it - light, sound, control. They tried to plant their feet against the raging wind but it was for nothing. They were ripped from the building like rag dolls stolen by a bully. Mark grabbed onto the railing outside, it took all his strength to pull himself and Wendy back to a standing position. In front, the line of villagers had stopped. They too clung to the railing. The last leaves of autumn battling against the first winter winds.

They waited for Mikey to get to the front of the column before moving out again. He carried an old storm lantern above his head.

The bridge from earlier now had water running freely over it, the couple were forced to let go of each other in order to get across. At the other end, the last person to cross turned and helped the other the final few feet then they would re-join the group waiting patiently a few feet away.

The trip was painfully slow; every step seemed to put them in danger of being pulled out to the sea. They could hear it crashing against the rocks somewhere out in the darkness. At no point did they feel safe.

As the lights of the village grew closer, Mark was surprised to see Maggie's dog Cobhair following their heels. The animal seemed unaffected by the weather. He felt like laughing, knowing the dog was there actually made him feel a little better.

Slowly they deposited each member of their group in a house until they reached the Cairn's. As they walked through the gate towards the house, Mikey grabbed hold of Marks arm. He leaned in close to his face. He could smell the stench of cigarettes and alcohol on his breath.

'I wouldn't try and do too much exploring round here tonight', he growled. 'The storms just beginning and Leathan's own don't much like visitors.'

Mark took his arm and shoved him away.

'What do you mean?' he shouted, 'what's happened here?'

A malicious grin spread across the man's lips. He turned and walked back into the storm.

<u>11</u>

Mikey gripped the rail as he walked back up the row of houses. He thought about the new couple. They'd no idea what was going on in Leathan. They'd gotten more courtesy in one hour than he had in his entire time here.

Mikey thought about the woman. Wendy. He thought about taking her back to his bolt hole he'd been allowed him to sleep in these past fifteen years. No nice village house for him.

He stopped as a wave crashed over the street, soaking him in the process. He tried not to look at the faces staring at him. They looked angrier than usual.

He waited for waves to die back before moving again. He looked into the window of Grath's house as he passed. She and the old woman Maggie were arguing about something.

Mikey struggled up and over the bridge, the water surged over it, he felt his feet pulling from underneath him, he gripped the hand rail tighter. Roaring wind tore at his raincoat. Something wasn't right. He'd been through storms before; there was something about off about this one.

He could feel the faces staring at him from behind. Hateful eyes boring into his back.

Mikey passed his one room bolt hole and went straight to the church. He'd pick himself up something to drink for the night.

He undid the heavy iron latch to the church. Inside was dry and dusty a few candles still guttered in the back giving off enough light for him to see.

He shuffled through the crates to the main hall where they'd just left. The fire had burnt down to a few ruddy embers. It cast wavering shadows around him. The wind rattled the door's hinges, like it was trying to get into the hall with him.

For the first time in years, Mikey felt cold, right down to his bones. Something was wrong.

He picked up a half-empty bottle of wine from the nearest table and took a long swig. A few more like that and he knew he'd feel fine again. He walked around looking for some more bottles but they were all empty. He'd have to go into the store rooms in the back for a full one. The thought made him uneasy but it had to be done.

Mikey turned when he heard footsteps behind him. There was nothing there but his own hazy shadow. He stood silently, gripping the bottle in his hand. Behind him he heard more steps, further away this time. Something moved slowly out of the corner of his eye.

Maybe he could get through the night with just the half bottle.

He turned to leave when he saw it was simply the door at the back of the hall.

'Just the wind!' he said out loud.

Mikey walked over to close it when he heard more footsteps from behind the door. They moved slowly, deliberately.

'Who's there?' he shouted, peering into the gloom.

He heard another set of footsteps join the previous pair. Then they were joined by another set, and another.

'Who is that? Show yourself!'

They stopped.

Shapes began to appear out of the shadows, and moved menacingly towards the open door. He could see their bright eyes peering at him. Panicking he slammed the heavy wooden door shut, dropping the bottle of wine in the process. The remnants of the bottle gathered in a dark pool next to him.

He staggered back before turning for the door. He stopped, horrified. Shadows swayed slowly in the dying flames of the fire, their bodies flickering nervously as if the wind were trying to blow them away.

'Leave me alone!' he screamed.

He turned to run but slammed into one of the tables and fell to the floor. Wine bottles crashed on to the floor around him. He looked up. The shadows seemed to detach themselves from the walls. They stood in a circle around him. Shards of glass pierced his hands as he tried to scrabble backwards away from them.

Suddenly he felt the salty wind pick up around him. He couldn't move against it, it was pulling him back towards the door. It stood wide open. The darkness beyond reached out for him

Mikey started to scream.

His hands left bloody smears on the floor as the shadows writhed like an uncontrollable bonfire before they all disappeared into the darkness.

<u>12</u>

Mr Cairns sat sipping his whisky.

He looked up at Mark.

'I don't know what you're expecting to hear from me' he said. 'It's been a long time since anybody confided anything to me in this village.'

They were sitting in the living room; a bottle of whisky lay between them on the table.

Wendy had gone to the bedroom. She said she wasn't feeling well again.

Mark needed some answers.

'Mrs Grath…' he started.

'…Grath is delusional' cut in Mr Cairns. 'She thinks she can keep this place going the way her mother did but it's been too long. The woman did something she never should've and now we have to live with it.'

'What happened, what did her mother do?'

'What she knew best' replied Mr Cairns. 'She cleaned. They were put away. "Out of sight, out of mind" she used to say.

'It wasn't until she died that the problems started. Nothing major at first, accidents for the most part; after a while they started happening more frequently. Usually to the folk who tried to leave.

'People would come, like yourselves. Some even tried to move in but soon enough rumour spread. The people couldn't have any children. They'd miscarriage or worse before a few months had passed.

'People started whispering 'curse' but Mrs Grath would bad mouth them until they either slunk off ashamed or remained guilt ridden for the rest of their time.'

'Is that what happened to you?' asked Mark.

The old man stared down into his empty glass.

'We tried so many times to have a child,' said Mr Cairns, 'every time something happened. We wanted to leave, start fresh somewhere else but we were so scared.'

Mr Cairns refilled his glass.

'I was the weak one, I should have taken us out of here but I didn't.'

'What about the other villagers?' asked Mark.

'Mrs Grath thinks everybody is either content or ignorant. The truth is they *are*. We've all lived here obeying her rules for so long I think we're all just used to it. You saw us all this evening, there's not a decade left in any of us… maybe that's how it should be..'

Mark sat quietly, thinking. Wendy came back into the room. She looked tired and drawn.

He took her hand and made her sit down in the chair next to him.

'You're looking tired do you want to take a nap, maybe you'll feel better after?'

She yawned in agreement. He bent over and pulled a blanket over her. Within minutes, she was sound asleep.

He turned back to Mr Cairns. The old man sat snoring in his chair, his glass still clutched between his frail hands.

Mark switched the lights off in the room and put his rain coat back on, took a deep breath and pulled open the door.

<u>13</u>

The storm threw Mark around like a twig as he made his way back up the village. The salt stung his eyes and got into his mouth with every set of waves that battered him. He clung to the freezing cold railing that ran along length of the village. The rain made getting a proper grip nearly impossible. He found himself holding on with his shoulders as well as his hands.

A bolt of lightning struck somewhere in the harbour, the whole village lit up. Mark thought he felt the hair on the back of his neck sizzling.

Another bolt came down even closer, down by the church. For a second he thought he could see the air crackle around him.

Mark stopped to try and catch his breath, a wave crashed over the beach and up to the walkway. He felt his feet slide from under him. He clung to the metal with all his strength.

As he pulled himself back to his feet a figure was standing in front of him. It was unaffected by the wind or waves crashing over it. The elements seemed to be washing right through it. Bright eyes stared menacingly down at him from underneath its hood.

Mark raised his hand up to it when another wave blinded him. As the water cleared from his eyes, the figure was gone.

Wiping the water from his eyes he looked around. He was all alone on the path but he didn't feel it. He looked around. Somewhere those cold dead eyes were still boring into him.

The shadowy presence had left him feeling colder then he'd ever felt.

Mark felt a sense of dread building up in his stomach.

He peered up ahead, he was nearly there.

He took a fresh grip on the rail and moved on. Whatever was out there was still staring at him, he could feel it.

It felt like hours instead of minutes but he reached the place he knew he could get some answers.

***

Mrs Grath's lights were still on.

Mark staggered up to the door and knocked. Nobody answered. He knocked again and heard a dog barking on the other side. Finally the door opened a crack and Maggie peered out.

'What the hell are you doing here? Maggie shouted.

She yanked open the door and pulled him inside.

'You think this is a joke? She pointed wildly outside at the raging storm. 'Have you not heard everything we've told you?!'

Mark held his hands up, the heat from the fire blasting him in the face. He was breathing hard.

'Listen,' he panted. 'I need some answers… my wife needs answers.'

He leaned against the wall, exhaustion hitting him.

'Everybody has a warning for us but nobody will tell us what we should be afraid of. What's going on here Maggie? What's wrong with Leathan?'

Maggie stopped and looked him up and down.

'The doors, the tunnels, the footsteps,' Mark said quietly 'What are they. What did you all do?'

Maggie's shoulders slumped; she suddenly looked a hundred years old.

She bent down and stroked Cobhair on his nose.

'He's taken to you' she said. 'You're the first person in years he's shown any interest in other than me.'

She smiled at the dog. He wagged his tail in response.

'It wasn't your fault. You really shouldn't have come here though. Not to Leathan. Not at this time. Things are always worse during storms. They're always restless.

The room was freezing. Mark could feel his whole body shaking but he couldn't rub his hands fast enough to get warm.

Maggie's breath steamed in the air in front of her.

The old woman looked around her. Her face looked regretful, apologetic.

'They're coming for you, and your beautiful wife. The cold comes when they do.'

'Who?' shouted Mark, 'who brings the cold with them Maggie?'

'Our fathers. Our children. We didn't expect them to take notice of you so soon. I think it's your wife's child.'

Mark looked at the old woman, confused.

'Wendy's not pregnant,' he said.

'Yes she is. We spotted it almost immediately. You're wife isn't ill Mark, she's just expecting.'

Mark could feel his heart pounding in his chest.

'You're wrong,' he said to Maggie, 'she would have told me.'

I wouldn't be surprised if she'd only found out recently herself dear. It's been a long time since we had a wee one round here, it's bound to attract a lot of attention.'

Mark remembered the conversation back at the Cairns'.

'Please, we have to get out of here. Mr Cairns said…'

Mark turned and reached for the door. Suddenly the house lurched as if someone had hit it with a hammer.

Mark fell to the floor.

Maggie had fallen back onto a chair, her face mirrored his. Shock.

'What's happening?' he shouted.

The house started shaking again. A window broke and then the storm was all around them. Furniture flew around the room, vases smashed against the wall and pictures rattled on their hooks. Water started to pour in from beneath the front door.

Mark felt something smash into the back of his head, he clutched where it struck. His hand came away bloody.

Maggie had climbed down onto the floor and was crawling towards the hallway door.

'It's happening again' she screamed over the wind. Why is it happening again?'

Grimacing against the pain, Mark began to crawl after her but the wind flipped the table over, barring his way.

'Maggie' he shouted. 'Maggie, what do we do?'

Maggie turned to him, bleeding from a cut on her brow and tears streaming down her cheeks. She tried to say something but the door behind her opened. Mark could see the hallway beyond, the door to the cliff face was open and a figure stood in the entrance. It reached its hand out to them.

Mark watched as Maggie was jerked violently back towards the door, her body twisted and bent like a rag cloth. She reached out for a handhold but it was too late. Her body was being pulled through the doorway into the darkness, the echo of her scream taken away by the wind.

Mark was on his own. The wind had died down. He crawled over to the window. The tide had come up over the harbour walls and flooded the street. There was no leaving the house that way.

He looked back towards the hallway. Light from the back shone steadily; menacingly stark against the chaos around him.

Mark picked his way through the room, past the remains of tables and chairs, shattered by the force of the wind. The water was now up to his knees. His foot caught on something as he moved. It was Maggie's cane, he picked it up and the added weight made him feel a little better.

Something cold touched his hand, he raised the cane to strike, at the last moment realised it was Maggie's dog, Cobhair. The dog barked once and then walked into the hallway, down towards the room at the back. Mark followed the animal.

Outside, the village was slowly being taken over by the sea. One by one, the houses were submerged, all traces of their past occupants washed away. Soon, Leathan would be no more.

14

The tunnel system behind Leathan twisted and turned, so that Mark had no idea where he was. He'd found a working torch outside the entrance but its pin prick of light was fighting a losing battle with the surrounding darkness

He'd followed the dog down the path from the main door and found nothing.

Mark couldn't stop thinking about Wendy. He'd left her with the Cairns and was mad at himself for it. He should never have left her alone. The final image of Maggie disappearing through the door haunted him.

He wouldn't let the same thing happen to his wife.

Mark tried not to think about Maggie's last words to him. Something was back here and all he had was a wooden cane and an

old dog if he was to come across
something.

He stopped to catch his breath, the tunnel
had started to go upwards and cold air
swept down over them. He was trying to
rub some warmth into his chest, when he
noticed Cobhair's ears go up. Mark
stopped to listen.

Something was walking ahead of them,
footsteps on gravel.

His breath caught in his throat.

It was clearer now. The footsteps were
joined by others, a whole group walking
together.

'The other villagers?' wondered Mark.

He took a step forward but Cobhair was
blocking his way. The animal let out a low
growl.

Mark pushed past the dog and up the
tunnel. Cobhair followed slowly behind.

They rounded a bend and found a kind of crossroads.

Mark stopped to listen out for the footsteps, but there was nothing but the wind.

He crept closer to the tunnel going up. There was a dim light flickering at the far end of the path.

Suddenly Cobhair let out a sharp bark and ran ahead. Mark called to the dog but it was too late. It had disappeared. He started up the tunnel himself.

He found the source of the flickering light – a candle in a chiselled hole in the wall, the first of many

There was still no sign of Cobhair. Mark hoped the dog had enough sense to find a way out.

The candles hissed and spat as the now constant wind blew them to and fro. The shadows danced manically, moving round him in circles. They'd fade in and out between each sconce but would never totally disappear. It was like they were watching his every step.

Mark rounded a bend. Before him was a large cavern, and he wasn't sure if it was man made or natural but it was vast. More candles adorned the walls. Inside was bare but for a table in the centre of the room.

Maggie's dead body lay on top of the table. Her hands crossed over her chest as in peaceful rest.

Mark realised he was shivering. It couldn't have been that cold with the candles but he felt frozen. He felt a gust of air pass through him, the cold gripped hold of him a little more.

He felt it closing in on him, wrapping itself tighter around his body. He tried to suck in a breath of air but found he couldn't. He fell to his knees, gasping. Shadows were closing in around him. It was getting so dark.

15

Mark woke up shaking, his bones felt frozen and candle light flickered around him. He tried to move again but his arms were like lead weights.

Another body lay next to him. Wendy. She was alive and he felt a surge of relief flood through his body.

The walls around them were chiselled from the same stone as the tunnels. Moss grew in the corners making the rooms look diseased.

There was an opening next to them that led to another candlelit area.

The same smell of decay seemed to hang around them. He couldn't tell if it was coming from something nearby or if it was the stone itself.

At first he thought it was the flickering candles playing tricks on him. Shadows resembling men faded in and out around them.

Mark looked back to Wendy. Her eyes were open and she was trying to move. She opened her mouth to speak but all that came out was a puff of frozen breath.

He could only watch as she struggled against her own body. Tears streaked down his cheeks, freezing as they hit the ground.

She stopped moving.

Mark held his breath, fearing the worst.

Wendy opened her eyes and looked straight at him. He smiled. The panic attack was over.

The room grew darker as another shadow stood in the doorway.

It was dressed in one of the heavy raincoats they'd seen earlier in the church.

The figure walked over to them slowly and kneeled.

Mark heard Wendy's breath catch.

'Hello there.'

They knew the voice. It was Mrs Grath.

'Try not to move too much, you'll loosen up shortly and we'll get you out of there.'

Mark tried to reply but his tongue was sandpaper on the roof of his mouth.

'Quiet now,' said the older woman, 'try not to draw too much attention to yourselves. This is a peaceful place and we don't like too much fuss.'

She turned to face the shadows of the room. She whispered something that Mark couldn't make out. Then she got up and left the room, and the shadows seemed to follow her out.

Slowly Mark could feel life coming back to his limbs. As the blood started circulating again, his legs began to tingle.

He turned to Wendy, who was on her side, her own body coming back to life.

'Are you alright? whispered Mark.

Wendy nodded. She moved her arm over to him and took his hand; it was freezing. The air around them was stale, as if they were lying in cold storage.

'It's them,' she whispered. 'They bring the cold with them.'

Mark nodded.

'Maggie told me,' he said. 'The dead of the village bring the cold with them. That's what we're feeling. Mrs Grath's mother did something when she put them all in here.'

He stopped and looked around.

'We need to get out of here,' he said.

284

'Mrs Grath told us to stay,' whispered Wendy, 'what if they come after us?'

'We can't,' said Mark. 'I don't trust Grath, I think I can find a way back out. But we have to go now.'

They stood silently for a second trying to get their balance.

They were both cold to the bone. He wasn't sure how far they'd make it but they had to try. Wendy looked in a worse state but she smiled at him reassuringly.

Holding each other up, they made for the doorway; it led down a short candle lit hallway and opened up to the large cavern Mark had seen earlier. Maggie's cane lay on the ground on the far side of the room. He must have dropped it when he collapsed.

Maggie still lay on the table. A blanket now covered the body. He turned Wendy away from it before she saw anymore.

'Don't look,' he said, 'it's Maggie, she was killed by whatever lives here. I think she was trying to warn me when it happened.'

'Did you see what happened?' whispered Wendy.

'I'm not sure, she was there one minute and gone the next but I heard her…'

Arm in arm, they continued for the entrance on the other side of the cavern.

Suddenly shadows appeared on the wall next to them. They moved angrily back and forth. Flecks of light burned coldly where their eyes should have been. A gust of wind swept through the cavern making the candles dance.

Then the shadows stepped from the wall in one sickening movement. The bodies appeared solid one minute, translucent the next. Except their eyes. They never left them.

286

'I told you to stay where you were,' said a voice from the opposite door.'

Mrs Grath stepped out of the darkness.

'I can't help you now.'

The circle of shadows tightened around them, forcing them towards the wall. Their gaze took on a look of desperate hunger.

Mark felt the cold creeping up his legs again.

'What did you do?' shouted Wendy at the old woman.

Mrs Grath stood primly.

'What we had to. My mother preserved the village. That's what was important. You would never understand.'

'This isn't preserving!' shouted Wendy. 'You made a hell for people to live in and now being swallowed up by the people you loved.'

Mrs Grath's eyes turned to stone.

'Leathan is gone, Mrs Grath' said Wendy.
'All that's left is you and…'

She looked at the dark figures surrounding
them.

Mrs Grath looked down, sadness showing
on her face.

'Maggie knew the truth of it' said Mark
'didn't she? That's why they took her. It's
only you now.'

Mrs Grath looked up and walked over to
the table in the centre of the cavern. She
pulled back the blanket and took Maggie's
dead hand in her own.

'Maggie was never really from Leathan,
she never agreed with what went on here. I
tried to tell her to watch what she said or
they'd come for her. She never listened.

Mrs Grath turned back to Mark and
Wendy.

'You're wrong about one thing though; it's not only me now. It's the three of us.

Suddenly a violent rumble ripped through the cavern, the walls began to shake, and the candles fell from their sconces and rolled across the floor.

The dead of the village continued to move towards them, the light in their eyes closing in. Mrs Grath held onto the table for support.

The cavern crumbled down around them. From somewhere down the tunnel, they started to hear a deep roar.

Something was coming.

A sudden wall of water burst from an opening. White froth bubbled and churned its way into the cavern. They all looked in shock as the sea poured in around them.

Amongst the raging tide, the drowned bodies of the remaining villagers tumbled through entrance. Their frozen frames eddied around their legs, catching onto their clothing.

Wendy screamed.

Mark grabbed her wrist and pulled her towards the door. He grabbed Maggie's cane off the floor of the cavern as they ran. The sea kept pouring in and the whole place would be underwater within a matter of minutes.

Mark pulled a candle down from one of the sconces and handed it to Wendy. He looked back. The shadows were following them into the tunnels.

<u>16</u>

Mrs Grath watched as the couple fled and she moved to the centre of the cavern. The water was up to her knees now. The ghosts of the village children surrounded her. They wanted their own time with the old woman now. She felt the cold climb up her body as they came closer.

She looked down fondly at them but all she got in return were burning vengeful eyes.

She was theirs now.

17

The water was deeper further down the tunnel. Mark clenched his teeth as the cold bit through his trousers. Light from Wendy's candle flickered across the water. Cold dead eyes followed them in the dark, but he couldn't tell how close they were.

The tunnel was getting steeper. Sweat poured off Mark's brow and he prayed he'd chosen the right path. The ghosts couldn't have been more than a few feet behind and Wendy was beginning to slow.

Wendy sucked air into her lungs, her chest was burning and she felt a sudden pain in her stomach. She could feel the ghosts behind her, reaching out for her. It was all she could do to keep moving.

She looked over her shoulder. They were within an arm's reach now, their eyes following her every move. She held onto Mark tightly. He was hitting the cane against the wall, three short bursts each time. From up ahead, she heard a familiar barking.

Mark breathed a sigh of relief, Cobhair had stayed close by. They found the dog up to its chest in water.

'Good boy,' said Mark patting the dog. It moved to Wendy and barked sharply at the darkness behind her. The dog turned and ran up another tunnel.

They followed Cobhair, trusting the dog's sense of smell. Mark took the rear and immediately felt the hollow cold come up from behind. He could feel the heat sapping out of his bones. He tried his best to push forward, but just then he could feel icy fingers groping his arms.

Wendy thought she could smell grass and the sea air. Not a hint of the death they'd left behind.

She rounded a bend towards a shaft of light shining down the tunnel, but came to a sudden stop as she hit solid wood.

The exit to the tunnel was blocked by an old gate. Cobhair scratched at the wood manically. Wendy pushed at the gate but it wouldn't budge. She rammed it with her shoulder again, still nothing. She could feel the cold creeping up behind her again.

She wedged her hand between some of the slats and pulled. She heard a sharp splintering and one of the planks gave way with a loud screech as the nails pulled free. Outside she could see blue sky. She took hold of another slat but it wouldn't move. She felt icy fingers pulling her back. And then Mark was there. He came crashing up from behind, throwing his full weight against the wood. Shards flew everywhere as his body pushed through. Fresh air and bright light flooded into the tunnel. Mark lay on the ground outside, not moving.

Wendy followed, it was like breathing the first air after being under water too long. She grabbed Mark's hand and pulled him further away from the tunnel exit, then fell onto the ground holding him between her legs.

She looked back through the gate to the dark tunnel. There was nothing there.

She saw that they were lying in Maggie's back garden, the edge of the cliff just behind them.

Cobhair came up behind her, sniffed at Mark's hand, and then stared to whine.

'We're out Mark… Mark!!…' she cried into his shoulder.

He never moved.

Wendy took Mark's head onto her lap, and turned his face to hers. His skin and lips were sickly blue and cold to the touch. His eyes stared glassily back at her.

Epilogue

Years passed and Wendy never told anyone what really happened on their anniversary trip; a tragic accident had taken her husband and that was it.

Eight months later she had a son. He was named after his father and was raised in Edinburgh. The boy grew up with an old dog called Cobhair that never left his side until it too died.

On his twentieth birthday, his mother took him on a trip to the north of Scotland. They parked the car beside the ruins of a small house. Mark helped his mother out of the car and they walked around the ruin.

He wasn't sure why his mother wanted to come all the way here. It really *was* in the middle of nowhere. He left her round the front of the house and walked along the path to the edge of the cliff. Far below, the sea crashed against the bluff, and for a moment he thought he saw something underneath the water. Strange, it looked like a row of houses. The waves covered it as quickly as they'd revealed.

He wandered back over to his mother, who was standing now at the back of the house and staring out to sea. She walked with a cane that she'd had for years. He always knew where she was by the noise it made when it hit the ground.

Mark hadn't noticed the broken gate at the back of the house, which swung back and forth in the wind, clacking against the back wall.

'Mum, you ok?' he asked.

She didn't answer. Mark pulled his jacket closer round him. It felt like winter had come early here. He put his arms around his mother and kissed her on the cheek.

'Come on, It's cold here. Let's go back to that café down the road. Have a cup of tea.'

His mother smiled up at him, a look of sadness in her eyes.

'Yes, that would be nice.'

They headed back to the car. His mother looked around when they got to the door. She had dropped her cane.

'Don't worry,' Mark said, 'I'll get it.'

He ran back round the house, to where the cane was lying in the grass. He stopped in front of the broken gate.

A light flickered in the darkness of the old house, and he stepped closer to look but a gust of wind swung the gate closed. He peered again towards the cottage, but the light had gone and all that was left was the darkness.

He picked up his mother's cane and returned to the car. They drove back down the path and onto the main road.

END

UPCOMING BOOKS IN THIS SERIES:

The Capitals Trilogy

The Islands Trilogy

All titles available in paperback and from most online e-book sellers.

www.wildwoodspublishing.co.uk

twitter @wildwoodsbooks

facebook.com/wildwoodspublishing

ABOUT THE AUTHOR

John Thoumire resides in Scotland. His first play was performed at the Traverse Theatre in 1995. He lives in Edinburgh with his wife Leisha and their dog, Fred.